BAD INTENTIONS

Karin Fossum began her writing career in 1974.
She has won numerous awards, including the
Glass Key Award for the best Nordic crime novel,
an honour shared with Henning Mankell and Jo
Nesbo, and the *Los Angeles Times* Book Prize.
Her highly acclaimed Inspector Sejer series has
been published in more than thirty countries.

ALSO BY KARIN FOSSUM

KARIN FOSSUM

Bad Intentions

TRANSLATED FROM THE NORWEGIAN BY
Charlotte Barslund

VINTAGE BOOKS
London

Published by Vintage 2011

4 6 8 10 9 7 5 3

Copyright © Karin Fossum 2008
English translation copyright © Charlotte Barslund 2010

Karin Fossum has asserted her right under the Copyright, Designs
and Patents Act 1988 to be identified as the author of this work

First published with the title *Den onde viljen* in 2008 by J. W.
Cappelens Forlag AS, Oslo

First published in Great Britain in 2010 by
Harvill Secker

Vintage
Random House, 20 Vauxhall Bridge Road,
London SW1V 2SA

www.vintage-books.co.uk

Addresses for companies within The Random House Group Limited can
be found at: www.randomhouse.co.uk/offices.htm

The Random House Group Limited Reg. No. 954009

A CIP catalogue record for this book
is available from the British Library

ISBN 9780099535843

This translation has been published with the
financial assistance of NORLA

The Random House Group Limited supports The Forest
Stewardship Council® (FSC®), the leading international forest
certification organisation. All our titles that are printed on
Greenpeace approved FSC® certified paper carry the FSC®
logo. Our paper procurement policy can be found at
www.randomhouse.co.uk/environment

Typeset by Palimpsest Book Production Limited,
Falkirk, Stirlingshire

Printed and bound in Great Britain by
CPI Bookmarque, Croydon CR0 4TD

CHAPTER 1

The lake, which was commonly known as Dead Water, lay like a well between steep mountains, and anyone who tried to wade into it would sink up to their knees in its soft mud. On the shore, partially hidden by spruce trees sat a small log cabin. Axel Frimann was looking out of the window. It was almost midnight on 13 September and the moon cast a pale blue light across the water. There was something magical about it all. At any moment, Axel imagined, a water sprite might rise from the depths. Just as the image came to him, he thought he saw a ripple in the water as though something was about to surface. But nothing happened and a smile, which no one noticed, crossed his face.

He turned to the other two and suggested that they should go rowing. 'Have you seen the light?' he said. 'It's really cool.'

Philip Reilly was reading. He tossed his long hair.

'Yes, why not?' he said. 'A trip on the lake. What do you say, Jon?'

Jon Moreno was lost in the flames in the fireplace. The fire made him feel warm and dizzy. In his hand he held a blister pack of anti-anxiety pills and every four hours he pressed one through the foil and put it in his mouth.

Did he want to go out on the lake?

He looked at Axel and Reilly. There is something about their eyes, something evasive, he thought, but then again, I'm not quite myself, I'm ill, I'm taking medication, calm down, they're my friends, they just want what's best for me. But he did not want to go out on the lake, not in the middle of the night in the cold moonlight. He did not trust himself completely. In here by the

1

fire he felt safe, in here between the timber walls, in the company of his friends, because they were his friends, weren't they? He tried to catch Reilly's eye, but Reilly had got up and was fumbling with something on a shelf.

'It's important that you get some exercise,' Axel said. 'Sitting still only makes your anxiety worse. You need to get your blood circulating, get it delivering oxygen to your cells. So come on.'

Jon did not want to let them down. They were doing this for him, they wanted him to have some fun and he did not have much of that at the hospital. Only endless days where nothing ever happened, spent wandering up and down the corridors. They were smiling at him, encouraging him now, Axel with his dark eyes, Reilly with his grey ones. So he got up from the chair and put the blister pack in his pocket. He never went anywhere without it. He reached out for his mobile which lay on the table, but changed his mind. His anxiety hummed through his body like an electric current. Somewhere a demon is flicking a switch, on and off, on and off, he thought, and I can't breathe.

'Put your jacket on,' Axel said. 'It's chilly.'

Jon looked around for his jacket. He could not remember where he had put it, but Axel found it and brought it over. Reilly blew out the paraffin lamp and a sudden darkness descended upon them. Jon knelt down to lace up his boots. A knot and a bow followed by another knot. Axel and Reilly waited.

'What about the fire?' Jon asked.

'We won't be gone long, there's no danger,' Axel said. 'Come on.'

'Shouldn't we put the fireguard in front of it?'

Axel shrugged. 'All right.'

He disappeared into the kitchen and they heard him scrabbling. Then he returned with the fireguard and placed it in front of the fire. The cast-iron fireguard was decorated with two wolves baring their teeth.

Jon looked at the wolves and at his two friends.

'We ready to go then?' Axel said.

Reilly nodded. Jon stuck his hands in his pockets. Axel patted him on the shoulder. His hand was warm and comforting. Trust us, the hand said, we only want what's best for you, you're among friends.

It was Friday the 13th of September. They went out into the dark night and fetched the oars from the shed.

A narrow path led down to the shore of Dead Water.

CHAPTER 2

The boat lay bottom up among the reeds, green and swollen like a pea pod. Axel and Reilly took hold of it and turned it over. It was filthy and slimy on the inside and by the light of the moon they saw a reptile scurry over the side and disappear.

'A lizard,' Axel remarked.

Jon stood with his hands in his jacket pockets. He stared at the boat with apprehension. He did not want to sit on the dirty thwarts. Axel read his mind and wiped them with the sleeve of his jacket.

'Sit at the stern,' he ordered him.

Obediently Jon stepped into the boat. He looked down at the black water. Perhaps there was no bottom, only mud that went on for ever. It might be good to let yourself sink, he thought, stop the fear flowing through your body for good. An explosion in his head, a burning sensation in his lungs and it would be all over. Axel and Reilly pushed off and the boat glided smoothly through the reeds. Jon felt it rock from side to side. He sat very still on the thwart, a skinny lad with small hands. His gaze wandered across the landscape, the steep mountains which surrounded the lake. Axel and Reilly each took an oar, fumbling at first until they found their rhythm. The boat gained speed.

'Look at the light,' Axel said.

The moonlight was cold and pale. Everything around them had acquired a metallic sheen. Reilly concentrated on rowing. The boat moved steadily across the lake, the water dripped like silver from the oars. Jon gripped the thwart with both hands. He was surrounded by darkness and black water. His fear gnawed at him like a sharp tooth.

Axel broke the silence.

'And what about your psychologist, Jon? Can you talk to him?'

'Her,' Jon corrected him. 'Her name's Hanna Wigert. Yes, I can talk to her.'

'How old is she?' Axel wanted to know.

'Forty, I think,' Jon said. 'Besides, she's a psychiatrist.'

'Same thing, isn't it?' Axel declared.

'No,' Jon said. 'It's not the same thing.'

The men rowed with long, steady strokes.

'And you talk about whatever you like?' Axel probed.

Jon looked the other way. 'I suppose so. Mostly about when I was little,' he said. 'But it wasn't when I was little that things went wrong.'

He felt disoriented. In the moonlight Axel's face was blue and white, and his eyes were black hollows.

'But your dad left you,' Axel said. 'That couldn't have been easy?'

Jon curled up on the thwart.

'People lose each other all the time,' he said, 'and they carry on anyway. As I did. It was fine, we managed fine.'

Axel's oar sliced like a knife through the water.

'Well,' he said, 'this is fun. But we all know what this is really about. Don't we, Jon?'

Everyone in the boat fell completely silent.

Jon's head dropped, he was having trouble breathing. Hanna had told him what to do when this happened. Stand up, she had said, so that your lungs have room to expand. But he was scared of standing up in the boat so he stayed huddled up, struggling to breathe.

Reilly mumbled a verse he had learned by heart.

'"If God were to punish men according to what they deserve, He would not leave on the back of the earth a single living creature: but He gives them respite for a stated Term: when their Term expires, verily God has in His sight all His Servants."'

'Jesus,' Axel said, 'I'm impressed. You know your Bible.'

'Koran, Axel, Koran.'

'Same thing, isn't it?'

'No,' Reilly said. 'It's not the same thing.'

Axel stuck his hand in his pocket and came up with a packet of Marlboro. The flame from the lighter made his face glow.

'Why are we stopping?' Jon asked.

'Just felt like a cigarette,' Axel replied.

Jon stared at his feet for a long time; he was feeling nauseous. He was far away from the cabin and even further away from the hospital. I'm in their way, he thought, I'm the weak link. I can't do what they can. Axel's eyes glow like his cigarette, those eyes will never leave me in peace.

Reilly stared at the bottom of the boat. He also seemed to be uncomfortable. He was too big overall, his arms and legs too long. His large hands rested on his knees. From the shore they heard a rustling sound, probably a bird taking off, Jon thought. Axel inhaled. Jon watched the repetitive movements. He followed the tip of Axel's cigarette with his eyes. It had an almost hypnotic effect on him. Why aren't they talking, he wondered, what are they waiting for? Are they trying to get rid of me, is that why they came to pick me up from the hospital, is that why they wanted to get me out here on the water, in the darkness? The fear crept up on him, but it was a ridiculous notion; they are my friends, he rebuked himself, sitting here worrying like a little kid, what am I thinking? Pull yourself together, Jon Moreno.

But he was incapable of pulling himself together. If only he could take off like the bird and fly away from everything, away from anxiety and guilt. Like a sleepwalker he got up from the thwart. Then he fell over the side of the boat.

Everything happened softly and quietly. There were only a few splashes which swiftly turned into ripples. Then he was gone.

Reilly leapt up, the boat rocked. He went to jump in after him, but Axel pulled him back down.

'Don't!' he shouted. 'You won't make it. You won't get him back into the boat, your clothes will get waterlogged and you'll both drown. Don't do it!'

'Jon can't swim,' Reilly screamed.

6

Axel held him tight. The boat settled down.

The water lay shiny and still.

They dragged the boat ashore.

Everything had happened so fast that Reilly had barely had time to think, but he was thinking now. And Jon must have thought, too, as he swallowed the cold, muddy water. While he sank to the bottom he must have been thinking that it was all over now. It was all over. But I'm still here, Reilly thought, and I wake up every day struggling to breathe. They were back inside the cabin. Axel lit the paraffin lamp. The fire had nearly gone out, only a few embers remained. He removed the fireguard with the two wolves and threw on a new log. It soon flared up. Reilly sat down on a chair. He slumped, his big hands resting on his thighs. It was not long before he rummaged around his inside pocket for a small bottle. It looked like the miniature shampoo bottles you find in hotels and it was filled with a clear liquid. He poured a little into the cap and swallowed it.

'What's that you're taking?' Axel wanted to know.

'An upper.'

'And what's an upper?'

Reilly closed his eyes.

'Don't worry about it. It's a substance which naturally occurs in your brain. I'm merely raising the level.'

He sat still, waiting for the rush which was about to hit his head and body. Soon he would feel as light as a feather. A wave would lift him upwards and onwards, and the pain which was always with him would melt away like snow.

'What are we going to do?' Reilly asked.

Axel waited a long time before he replied.

'I've got an idea,' he said. 'We do nothing right now. We wait until the morning, then we call. We say that Jon must have gone out while we were sleeping. That we woke up and found his room empty. It's simpler like that. It's the middle of the night and it would take them several hours to drive here. They can't start looking for him now, anyway. What do you think, Reilly?'

Reilly shook his head. 'We have to call,' he said. 'Who do we call, who will come?'

'Divers,' Axel said. 'Police officers and people from the rescue services. And they might bring dogs. It'll be teeming with people here. Also, I've been thinking about something,' he added. 'I don't fancy telling Ingerid that we watched Jon drown. I don't want to be a bigger part of this than I have to. It was Jon's choice.'

'But he didn't have a choice,' Reilly objected.

'He was ill,' Axel said.

Again there was silence in front of the fire. The rush carried Reilly off.

Besides, it suited him fine that Axel made the decision.

'We need to agree on some key points,' Axel said. 'I'm the first to wake up. I see that Jon has gone. I go straight to your room to tell you. I run around the forest calling out for him, but after one hour we give up and phone for help.'

'They'll want to know how Jon was,' Reilly said. 'If we noticed anything.'

'We didn't notice anything in particular. Jon was just as he always was. And we haven't found any letters. We need to roll out his sleeping bag, he didn't unpack it. We'll say that we went to bed at midnight and that we haven't seen him since.'

They went to the smallest bedroom, where Jon normally slept. Reilly rolled out the sleeping bag and arranged it on the bed. He pulled down the zip and rumpled it up a bit. Axel put his hand on Reilly's shoulder.

'Let's go and sit down, have a beer.'

'He went straight down,' Reilly said.

'I know,' Axel replied.

They were back in front of the fire. Reilly met Axel's eyes in the flickering glow.

'You're finding this all very convenient, aren't you? That he's gone.'

Axel clenched his teeth. 'I think you should watch your mouth,' he hissed.

'I've noticed how you look at him sometimes,' Reilly said. 'I think Jon found you intimidating. I think he felt you were always judging him.'

'Your imagination is playing tricks on you,' Axel said. 'No more drugs now, they mess with your mind. You need to have a clear head tomorrow when the police turn up.'

They sat in silence for a while.

'Why don't we make the call now?' Reilly said. 'Why don't we call for help right away?'

Axel got up and started wandering around the room. 'Taking your own life is a choice you make alone,' he said, 'and I do not want to be literally a spectator of it.'

'But we were spectators. And we'll have to talk to his mum. She'll ask all sorts of questions. She'll blame us for not taking better care of him.'

'That's why I want to tell the police another version,' Axel explained. 'He went out on his own. Everything was beyond our control, we were asleep. But we're obviously devastated. Do you think you can manage that?'

Reilly sent him a dark look.

'Yes,' he said. 'I can do devastated.'

CHAPTER 3

Reilly woke up early.

The light cut through a gap in the curtains and he shuddered as he recalled the night just past. He believed that Jon had died for him and Axel, that he had assumed the blame because he was the weakest, because he was the link that might break. But surely none of us deserves to die, he thought, we aren't bad people.

The day was coming through the window like a beam of light and it pinned him to the mattress. His first thought was to huddle against the wall, close his eyes and never get up, never deal with any of it. Instead he wriggled out of his sleeping bag, put on his old corduroy trousers and went into the living room. Axel Frimann was standing there staring out of the window.

'I went down to the lake,' he said.

'Why?'

'Just wanted to check that everything was all right.'

Reilly gave him a baffled look. His long hair was a tangled mess after the hours spent in bed. With his protruding chin and pointed nose he looked like a troll from a fairy tale.

'Nothing is all right.'

'Don't talk like that,' Axel said.

'But it's the truth.'

Axel sat down on the sofa and put his feet on the coffee table.

'We've talked about the nature of truth before,' he said. 'Many things are true, but they still need to be left alone. Imagine if people always told the truth, it wouldn't work. Society would fall apart. We need to start each day from scratch,' he argued. 'Build something that people can see, that they can cope with and believe in.'

'You can't speak for everyone,' Reilly said. 'Not everyone agrees with you.'

Axel gave him a challenging look.

'Then think about Jon's mum, when she finds out that she has lost him. Imagine how awful that will be. And imagine if she were to learn that her son was not the boy she thought he was and his memory was horribly tarnished. How would she cope with that? Don't talk to me about truth: people can't handle it. And they don't want to hear it, either. Listen to me!'

He leapt to his feet and went out into the kitchen. Reilly heard him clattering with the coffee pot and pouring water from a bucket. He went back into his bedroom and put on a T-shirt. He went over to the window and stared down at Dead Water, which lay there like a green and black mirror. Perhaps a layer of mud had already settled on Jon's skinny body and the divers would not find him with their torches. Jon was small and thin. Jon could be mistaken for a branch, a modest bump on the bottom.

He snapped out of his trance and left the cabin, but collapsed on the two large stones which served as the front steps.

Axel came outside.

'Calm down,' he said. 'Jon had been ill for a long time. We could see it coming.'

Reilly remained sitting with his head buried in his hands, incapable of speech. He badly needed something to calm him down, but Axel had banned him from getting high until it was all over and done with. The expression 'over and done with' echoed in his head as though they had committed a crime, as though they had personally pushed Jon out of the boat.

'Of course I've wondered about it,' Axel continued. 'I don't mind admitting it. What do you think Jon did at the hospital? He had therapy and he talked. He talked for four weeks. He was encouraged to open up about everything, the most intimate things that tormented him, that had led to his breakdown. The truth would have come out sooner or later. It would have taken us with it and we wouldn't be sitting here by the water now. Do you hear what I'm saying?'

'We don't know anything about what he did or how he would have handled it,' Reilly said. 'You're just guessing. People get through all sorts of things.'

Axel found a stick and began stabbing the ground in front of the steps.

'There's unlikely to be much fuss made over this,' he said. 'Jon had been admitted to Ladegården Psychiatric Hospital with anxiety and depression and he was on medication. The police will soon join the dots. Meanwhile, we need to cherish our freedom.'

'If that freedom is a torment,' Reilly said, 'then it's not worth much. You don't feel pain like other people,' he added.

He sat there staring into the forest. From where he was sitting the black spruce trees looked dark and mysterious. The light fell through the treetops in long, slanted columns. A pine had keeled over, roots spiking up dramatically amidst all the green like a claw. Then he spotted something between the trees, a flash of white. Axel followed his pointing hand.

'Someone's there,' Reilly said.

'Oh, shut up,' Axel replied.

Reilly panicked.

'What if someone saw us last night? There are bound to be more cabins up here, someone could have watched us through binoculars. It was a full moon.'

'The crows saw us,' Axel said. 'And they're bound to tell the magpies and the lapwings, and before you know it will be all over the forest.'

Reilly paced up and down on his long legs.

'Something's moving,' he stated. 'In the heather over there, to the right of the pine. There's definitely something moving.'

They crossed the area in front of the cabin, passed some scrub and peered in between the pines. Reilly sped up and started to run, his long hair fluttering like a horse's mane. On the ground, at the foot of a pine, lay a dead cat. And next to the cat, four kittens. They too were dead, but a fifth was crawling through the heather trying to get away.

Something happened to Philip Reilly. The sight of the helpless kitten moved him. He had never seen anything so small, so doomed as the tiny creature. The events of last night had shaken him and he melted like butter in the sun.

'Have you seen it?' he said. 'Poor thing.'

Axel watched in amazement as Reilly bent down and picked up the kitten, which was white with grey specks, with his big hands. From its toothless mouth a weak mewing could be heard. Its eyes were just about open, surprisingly blue, its tail a stump as thin as a piece of string.

'I'll take him inside,' Reilly said. 'He needs something to eat.'

Axel snapped his fingers in front of his face to rouse him.

'Listen,' he said, 'we have a lot of things to do. We need to make that call. You can't spend your time looking after a kitten now, are you out of your mind?'

Reilly paid no attention to him. He strode back to the cabin still holding the kitten. It weighed only a few grams. Reilly half closed his hand again. The kitten clawed his palm.

'Do we have any milk?'

'No,' Axel said. 'And cats aren't supposed to drink milk anyway, they need water, otherwise they get fat. And anyway, cow's milk is too hard for them to digest.'

'Fat?' Reilly opened his hand. 'Do you see how skinny he is? He weighs nothing.'

Axel walked past him and into the cabin. Reilly followed him. He held the creature like a freshly laid egg, his entire lanky, lumbering body focusing on the tiny animal. He opened a cupboard and rummaged among boxes and bags.

'Powdered milk?' he said.

'No,' Axel said.

'Condensed milk?'

'We don't have that either.'

Reilly was starting to look despondent.

'We didn't manage to save Jon,' he said, 'but we can save this one. One life for another. The Koran says so. We need a shoebox and a towel,' he added. 'Do we have a box?'

'Put it down,' Axel ordered him. 'We need to talk. We need to get our story straight. Could you concentrate for five minutes, please? Why did you bring the kitten inside? What were you thinking? Are you on something?'

Reilly ignored him.

'Water,' he said. 'Find a bowl. I'll make mush out of some bread-crumbs. You brought a loaf of bread, didn't you?'

He placed the kitten on the kitchen counter where it remained on wobbly legs. He found an empty cake tin decorated with Disney figures on the top shelf. He recognised Cinderella, Snow White and Pinocchio.

'This will be fine,' he said. 'This box is crying out for an inhab-itant.'

Axel was holding his mobile. He looked frazzled.

'The question is who do we call?' he said. 'The police or the hospital? Or his mum? What do you think, Reilly? Hello! Could you pay attention for a moment, please, I'm trying to save your skin!'

'Save my skin?' Reilly said.

'This would never have happened if you hadn't started talking about Islam,' Axel said. 'You said time was running out. You said judgment was approaching.'

'You were the one who wanted to go rowing,' Reilly said.

He turned away from Axel Frimann. He gave the kitten some-thing to drink. He found a tea towel on a hook and made a small nest in the cake tin. Then he carefully placed the kitten inside it. It coiled up instantly. For a while he admired the little animal, which had now quenched its thirst and settled down. He had been unaware that he had such a talent for care-giving. It was enor-mously inspiring.

'What do we do about its mother?' he said. 'And the dead kittens?'

'Who says you need to do anything about them?' Axel held out his mobile. 'Get real, will you?'

'But the fox will get them,' Reilly fretted.

'Of course. That's his nature.'

'We could cover them up. Or bury them.'

'The fox would sniff them out,' Axel said. 'You know that.'

Reilly admired the kitten in the cake tin. A grey and white ball of fluff on a chequered tea towel. A small furry miracle.

'You do the talking,' he mumbled. 'You know best.'

Axel rang the number of the hospital where Jon had been a patient for four weeks. His voice was filled with concern while he explained what had happened.

'We got up at nine,' he said. 'And discovered that his room was empty.'

CHAPTER 4

While they waited they wandered up and down the forest paths.

Reilly studied Axel and the way he walked. He strode around energetically as though rehearsing for a performance he was about to give. The role of the calm but concerned friend of Jon Moreno.

'I might have been able to pull him out,' Reilly said. 'If you hadn't stopped me.'

Axel dismissed it. 'Jon would have fought you,' he said. 'Besides, he was wearing a reefer jacket and thick lace-up boots, and you were wearing a knitted jumper as thick as a coat. We were a long way from the shore. We would not have been able to save him. It would have been impossible to lift a man into such a small boat, you would both have drowned. Shut the gate after you,' he added. 'There are sheep grazing here. I can hear bells.'

Reilly closed the gate with a twisted loop of wire. With heavy footsteps he followed Axel. The lake lay to their right, with its calm and black surface, and Jon lay on its bottom, his lungs full of water. Then he remembered the kitten and it all churned inside his head, the kitten and Jon, the kitten and Jon.

Philip Reilly was almost two metres tall and quite lean. He had long, sand-coloured hair which he left to grow as it pleased and he wore a full-length coat with big pockets.

'If I owned an orchard, you could get a job as a scarecrow,' Axel quipped.

Reilly did not react.

It was all right with him if Axel thought he looked like a scarecrow, he was not bothered. Besides, he was angry. He kicked the earth, sending sand and soil flying around his legs. Jon, he thought, Jon my man, Jon my mate.

'Don't take me down with you,' Axel said. 'I'm no villain and neither are you. You need to learn to look towards the future and you need to learn to assert yourself.' He gestured forcefully. 'Breathe out,' he said. 'And keep moving. Be a shark, for God's sake.'

Reilly did not reply. There was not much to say and it was fine that Axel was doing all the talking.

They had reached an old, rotten fence.

'Something's hanging on the fence,' Axel said. 'An old swimming costume. Do you see it?'

'It's mouldy,' Reilly said. 'Leave it alone.'

'A swimming costume,' Axel repeated.

It was yellow with black stripes. He snatched it and pulled at the elastic material.

'It's a wasp costume,' he said.

He kept pulling at the swimsuit.

'Can you imagine it, Reilly? A giant wasp cruising around the beach, scaring the living daylights out of everyone.'

'Jon is dead,' Reilly said. 'Stop messing around. We're not kids any more. What is wrong with you?'

Axel returned the swimming costume to the fence.

'You can cry,' he said, 'or you can play ball and save your life.'

Axel Frimann walked on. Whether you were male or female he was undeniably a joy to watch. His supple limbs were perfectly co-ordinated, his arms swung from his shoulders and his hips controlled his legs. He moved forwards with flexibility and elegance, at once lazy and purposeful. Reilly followed at a distance, his hair fluttering in the wind, his coat-tails flapping like a sail. His head did not know what his legs were doing, and he scrambled down the path as if someone had put boots on a bundle of logs.

Axel started listing the good intentions which had motivated them originally. What had followed was bad luck, pure and simple, and beyond their control. In a moment of weakness they had been tricked by one of nature's whims.

Axel talks and talks, Reilly thought. I've never had any goals or a purpose, but I've never hurt anyone. Now I don't know what to believe any more.'

Axel placed a hand on his shoulder.

'Repeat is the biggest advertising agency in Norway,' he said. 'I earn 750,000 kroner a year. I've waited for a job like this my whole life and no one is going to take it away from me.'

Reilly threw open his arms as though he was hanging from a crucifix.

'This will never end,' he objected. 'We'll have to live with it for the rest of our lives. And I don't know if I can manage that.'

'You can,' Axel said. 'Because you're not an old woman like Jon.'

Reilly was a man of peace, but he saw red. He ran back to the cabin and stormed into the kitchen to check on the kitten. It was still breathing.

CHAPTER 5

The cars were parked diagonally in a row on the grassy bank by the cabin. The sun was higher now and reflected in the windscreens. The fire brigade had turned up with two divers and an orange rubber dinghy on a trailer, the Red Cross with a dog and a search and rescue team. The dog was an Alsatian, sturdy and shaggy with black, intelligent eyes. The police had sent two men. Konrad Sejer was an inspector, and he had a striking presence. He was tall and slim with thick grey hair and lined features. Jacob Skarre was considerably younger with blond curls. The grass was crowded with men and women and Axel went to meet them. He was a man overcome by grief and anxiety, his voice carried on the wind. You could detect traces of anguish and vulnerability in it. Reilly studied the performance. He was impressed, but he had seen it before. Axel could put on a good show and it cost him nothing.

'We got up at nine and discovered that he was gone,' he said. 'It was a shock. He was in such a bad way.'

The inspector shook his hand. The handshake made Axel Frimann gasp.

'You've looked for him?' Sejer asked.

Axel nodded. 'We walked across the sheep fields and we called out for him. But all we found was an old swimming costume and it can't be Jon's. But we're more worried about the lake.'

He pointed in the direction of Dead Water.

Reilly stayed silent. It felt strange to hear these lies. As though they had pushed Jon out of the boat and were now covering up their crime. He examined Sejer and Skarre. Their names when spoken in the same breath sounded like a hedge trimmer, he thought. Even though they were face to face with the law and lying through their teeth, all he could think about was the kitten in the cake tin. It baffled him. It had taken root in his heart. It had attached itself there with its claws. I need to get high, he thought.

'Which one of you called the hospital?' Sejer asked.

'I did,' Axel said. 'I called the ward.'

'He had been given permission?'

'Until Sunday evening. We're old friends. We picked him up yesterday afternoon. We thought the change might do him good.'

Skarre took a step forward.

'Do you happen to know the name of his doctor?'

Axel and Reilly looked at each other. 'Now what was it?'

'Wigert,' Axel said. 'Hanna Wigert.'

Skarre noted it down. He seemed bright and energetic, or as Axel would have put it, eager to please. He raised his eyes towards the black lake.

'He might have gone for a walk,' he said calmly. 'A walk in the woods can do you good when it all gets too much.'

There was something about his eyes, something critical, which signalled that he would not allow himself to be deceived and would not automatically believe what they told him. Reilly grew nervous. The hedge trimmer could come down on them at any moment.

'We've been up since nine,' Axel said. 'He would not have gone far on his own. He scares easily.'

'Does he have a mobile?' Skarre asked.

'It's inside,' Axel said, 'and that's weird. That he didn't put it in his pocket, because he always does.'

Skarre turned to the divers who were leaning against the rescue vehicle.

'All right,' he called out. 'Let's get started.'

He fixed his glance on Reilly.

'Were you drinking last night?'

Reilly shrugged. 'We had a little wine. Jon was the first to go to bed, but he wasn't drunk, if that's what you were thinking.'

'I don't think anything,' Skarre said.

Then, having considered this for a moment, he asked: 'Are you missing anything?'

'What do you mean?' Axel frowned.

'Is anything missing?' Skarre explained. 'Did Jon Moreno take anything with him?'

'We haven't noticed anything missing,' Axel said.

Skarre issued instructions to the emergency team, and the divers started carrying their equipment down to the lake. Skarre himself joined Sejer in the cabin. Reilly followed. He went to the kitchen and lifted the kitten out of the cake tin. His hands were the size of plates. You could eat porridge out of them, Axel used to say. The kitten was lying there, curled up.

'Where did you find it?' Sejer said.

'In the forest,' Reilly said. 'The other kittens were dead. So was their mother. I brought it inside. There are foxes around here.'

'Yes,' Sejer said. 'They need to eat too.'

'It's not food,' Reilly said gruffly.

They sat down in front of the fireplace. Sejer wanted to know their names, dates of birth and where they worked. If they often came to this cabin at Dead Water, and why it was called Dead Water, did they know? Did they have a map of the area? No, Axel replied. He mostly asked questions about Jon. About how long they had known him. If he was depressed, if he had indicated that he might want to end it all. They said he had been quiet the whole evening, a little introverted, as though he was struggling with difficult issues. He pops anti-anxiety pills all the time, Axel explained.

'What's he scared of?' Sejer asked.

Axel was momentarily wrong-footed.

'This anxiety of his is complicated,' he said, 'because we don't know all the things that he worried about.'

'He was scared, but you never asked him what he was scared of?'

Axel and Reilly looked at each other.

'I don't think you quite understand anxiety,' Axel began.

'Yes,' Sejer said, 'I do. And I expect old friends to know one another. His pills, where are they? Did he take them with him?'

Reilly looked up from the kitten.

'He always keeps them in his pocket. Never goes anywhere without those pills. Not that they do him much good, in my opinion. Jon trembles like an old man. Like this.'

He held up his hand to demonstrate.

Sejer picked up a Nokia mobile phone lying on top of a pile of newspapers.

'Jon's mobile?'

The sight of the mobile made Reilly nervous. He got the feeling they had overlooked something. Perhaps it has to do with truth, he thought, it has its own quality which you cannot emulate, its own pure tone.

'So what do you think?' Sejer wanted to know.

'Well,' Axel said, 'we fear the worst. That he might have jumped into the lake. Last night. While we were sleeping.'

'Why would he have done that?'

'He was hospitalised. In a psychiatric ward.'

'Is that a reason?'

Axel smiled patronisingly. 'You probably don't understand what I mean,' he said.

'Can he swim?' Skarre asked.

'No,' Axel said. 'Jon can't swim.'

The search and rescue team was moving towards the lake.

Reilly followed Sejer and Skarre with his eyes. They acted as if they owned the place. The cabin, the grassy bank and the lake. There was something very organised about them, a sense of purpose which made him feel uneasy.

Sejer looked at the green boat, then across the lake.

'How deep is it?' he asked.

'Don't know,' Axel said.

'Have you touched the boat?'

'No.'

22

Sejer squatted down. 'I'm asking because I can see that someone has moved it,' he said. 'It used to lie higher up, there are marks in the grass.'

We did not see those, Reilly thought, because it was dark. We did not even think about them. That's it, we're going to get caught.

Sejer wandered up and down the shore; Skarre walked alongside him. They conferred quietly with each other.

'This is the only place you can wade into the water,' Sejer observed. 'If Jon walked into the lake, then this is where he did it. The rocks on the other side look inaccessible. Or what do you think?'

'How do you get up into the mountains?' Skarre asked.

'From the other side,' Reilly explained. 'It's a long way. And it's very steep.'

He closed his mouth. It was best to shut up and let the police draw their conclusions in peace. When the whole miserable business came to light one day, they would just have to deal with it then. Sejer talked to the divers and agreed on an approximate point where Jon might lie.

'If he's in the water at all. There are other possibilities,' Sejer said.

The rubber dinghy was launched and the divers waded into the water. The Red Cross team would search the forest area around the lake. Abel the Alsatian strained on his leash, keen to get going. The divers were now some distance out and one of them had gone under with a powerful torch. When their work was well under way and the search party had disappeared into the sheep fields, Sejer asked to see where Jon had been sleeping. They returned to the cabin. Axel opened the door to the smallest bedroom. The room was almost bare, with red gingham curtains, a small bedside table and a paraffin lamp. On the wall hung a photo of the King and Queen of Norway. Axel pointed to the sleeping bag. It was green with orange lining and lay in a messy heap on the foam mattress. A blue nylon bag was leaning against the wall.

'Is that Jon's bag?'

They nodded.

'What time did he go to bed?'

'It was around midnight. Or what do you think, Reilly?'

'Midnight,' Reilly mumbled.

'You said he was quiet last night? That he was quieter than usual?' Sejer asked.

'He was very depressed,' Axel explained, 'and has been for a long time: that was why he had been admitted to Ladegården. Jon is a worrier, he can't handle very much. We should not have let him sleep on his own,' he added. 'I don't know what we were thinking.'

A flash of anguish crossed his face. He is in control of every single muscle, Reilly thought.

'Do you know why he fell ill?' Skarre asked.

They shook their heads.

'People get ill,' Axel said. 'It happens.'

'Did it happen suddenly?'

'I suppose it was gradual.'

'And when did it start?'

Reilly felt like giving up right there and then. They would want to know everything. They would talk to Jon's mother and his friends, the staff at the hospital and his colleagues at Siba Computers, where he had worked over the past year, and everyone would add a piece to the puzzle. All the police would have to do was put them together.

I need to get high, he thought.

'It started last winter,' Axel said.

He had decided to tell the truth as far as possible. Other people would remember that was when it had started. It was a question of being one step ahead.

'He was having trouble sleeping. It must have been around Christmas. He lost weight. He was off sick from work. In spring it got worse; eventually he couldn't manage even the simplest things and he spent the whole summer in bed. We went to visit him a couple of times, but he turned his face to the wall and wouldn't talk to us. He was admitted four weeks ago. We've been so worried,' Axel said, 'and we don't know what's happened, but we fear the worst.'

'Let's not meet trouble halfway,' Sejer said.

'It usually works out all right,' Skarre said.

Four hours later they found the body of Jon Moreno.

The rubber dinghy was pulled ashore and the search in the forest was called off. The Alsatian padded over the grass, alert, its ears pricked up. Axel and Reilly went down to the lake to see Jon. Axel with the solemnity befitting a man in mourning, Reilly with downcast eyes and trembling hands.

Jon was lying on a stretcher. Never before had he looked so small, so defenceless. Reilly turned away and took a few steps towards the forest. Poor Jon. Consumed with guilt and shame. The next instant he felt bitter because he would have to bear this torment until the day he died. And even worse, it dawned on him, Ingerid Moreno would ask them to be pall-bearers. From now on they would have to pretend. They would have to fake it for the rest of their lives, weigh up every single word, calculate every gesture, every glance.

He stopped and looked back. It was not easy to see that it was Jon lying on the stretcher, it was just a skinny carcass with the face of a stranger. How much death takes from us, he pondered – warmth, colour and vitality. Now there is only wet, grey skin over sharp bones. Axel went over to the stretcher. He fell to his knees and mumbled a few words which the wind carried in Reilly's direction.

'Sorry, Jon, for not taking better care of you.'

They were told to come to the police station.

Axel closed the windows in the cabin and Reilly cleared up the rooms. All the way back to town he sat with the cake tin on his lap as he fretted about what the police would do to them. Axel insisted it would be a mere formality. Everything would be over and done with in a matter of minutes.

'What more can we say apart from what we've already told them?' he said. 'Jon went to bed around midnight and that was the last we saw of him. We've just simplified events. They can't pin anything on us. What evidence is there?'

Reilly stroked the kitten. They did not talk much the rest of the way because ultimately no words could express what had happened.

Three hours later they parked outside the police station. They had to wait in reception. Again Reilly voiced his concerns about everything that could go wrong.

'It'll be fine,' Axel reassured him. 'It's a straightforward story. It's impossible to screw it up.'

Reilly became aware of two people crossing the room. One of them seemed familiar. He gripped Axel's arm.

'It's Ingerid,' he whispered.

Reilly had known that this was something they would have to get through, but it was happening sooner than he had imagined, and he hadn't had time to prepare himself. Ingerid Moreno was accompanied by a female police officer and now she spotted them. She collapsed and started sobbing. Axel shot up from his seat.

'We didn't know he was in such a bad way,' he said. 'If we had known, we would have taken better care. And if the hospital had known about his intentions, they would not have given him permission to leave for the weekend. Ingerid. Listen to me. None of us could have foreseen this.'

Ingerid Moreno nodded and wiped away her tears. Reilly remained in his seat without saying anything. Ingerid did not appear to see him. She was caught in the light which always surrounded Axel. If Axel could act so convincingly, with such apparent sincerity, how often had he himself been deceived? What was the basis of their friendship? Was it all just one big lie, a star performance?

'You must come and visit me some time,' Ingerid pleaded. 'We need to talk. Please.'

'We'll come,' Axel said. 'There is so much we want to tell you. All the things we shared with Jon. Which you don't know about.'

'Tell me he was a good boy,' Ingerid begged. 'Tell me that he was a good person.'

'Yes,' Axel Frimann said. 'Jon was a good person.'

'It's possible that Jon Moreno took his own life,' Sejer said.

Axel and Reilly looked at him in amazement. His words were so unexpected that they gawped. Was he considering other options? Why would he do that? Was it an automatic response? Perhaps he instinctively thought they were dishonest because in the course of his work he was unaccustomed to meeting honest people? It struck them that this man never made assumptions, not even about an obvious suicide. And if he decided Jon's death had been a suicide, he would still want to know why it had happened and if it could have been prevented. If Jon had tried to kill himself before, if there had been warning signs, if they had ever discussed the subject of death and what, if anything, Jon had expressed. Anxiety, relief, longing. If he was taking something in addition to his prescribed medication, if he had said anything during the evening which had made them wonder.

'Think back,' he said. 'Go through everything that happened. What about the drive there in the car: did something happen on the way, did you stop anywhere?'

They had not expected such attention to detail. Calmly and methodically Sejer worked through the events of the past two days and Skarre noted down everything that was said.

'In cases such as this,' Sejer went on, 'we follow a procedure. It consists of a series of questions. We will come back to you when we have more information such as the autopsy report, and after other friends and relatives have been interviewed.'

Skarre had pushed his chair towards the wall. He exuded a boyish enthusiasm as though these routines had not yet started to affect or bore him.

'Let's talk about last night,' Sejer said. 'His final hours. Was he in a particular mood or had anything about him changed?'

'It was a quiet evening,' Axel said. 'We just discussed stuff as friends do.'

'Such as?'

'You want to know what we talked about?'

'Yes, please.'

'But why?'

'It's one of the questions we need to ask.'

Axel Frimann raised an eyebrow.

'We talked about films,' he said. 'We go to the cinema a lot and we have strong views about what we see.'

'Are you interested in acting?'

'I'm fascinated by it,' Axel admitted. 'All the roles we need to play. If we're good, we'll go far.'

'Are you good?' Sejer wanted to know.

Axel smiled a patronising smile.

'I do all right,' he said.

Skarre's pen raced across the pad. From time to time he looked up, alert.

'What about Jon?' Sejer asked. 'Could he play a role? Was he capable of acting?'

Axel hesitated.

'Jon was quite helpless,' he said. 'What can I say? He was at the mercy of reality. No shield. So I suppose the answer is no.'

'Can you tell me anything about Jon's reality?' Sejer asked.

Axel glanced towards Reilly for support, but he had lowered his head so that his long hair concealed his face like a curtain.

'You had better ask at the hospital,' Axel suggested. 'Ask his doctor. She must have found out something during the last few weeks.'

'I will talk to his doctor,' Sejer said, 'but I also need to ask his best friends. You were close, weren't you? What else did you talk about?'

'Ladegården Hospital. Jon told stories from the ward. It was funny.'

'How long was he there?'

'Four weeks.'

'You visited him there?'

'Yes.'

'Did he like it there?'

'He didn't have a choice,' Axel said.

They talked about Jon for an hour. When it was all over, Axel held out his hand.

'Please don't hesitate to get in touch if there is anything else,' he said.

CHAPTER 6

'Well, who would have thought it?' Jacob Skarre said. 'Frimann, Reilly and Moreno are in our system. And they have been since last December.'

Sejer leaned forward and read the screen.

'They were questioned as part of a missing person's case,' Skarre said, 'but it was just a routine interview. An odd coincidence. Or perhaps there's no such thing?'

'I'll have a look at the file,' Sejer said. 'But there's no reason to suspect that a crime has been committed, so we'll proceed on that basis. For now,' he added. 'And if there is a link, it'll show up eventually, don't you think?'

'It'll show up,' Jacob Skarre agreed.

Three days later they visited Axel Frimann in his flat. Axel was convinced that he had made a good impression on the two men. There were several factors which contributed to his credibility; his attractive appearance and broad shoulders were only two of them. He was eloquent too. He spoke with concern and restraint and most of the time he felt on top of the situation. Concealing details about Jon's suicide was a tiny act he had performed to spare Ingerid Moreno more painful knowledge. He directed Sejer and Skarre to the sofa while he pottered about because being active gave him a sense of control. Axel Frimann never relinquished power.

'When it comes to Jon's death,' Sejer said, 'there are a few details which baffle us. That's why we are here.'

Axel looked at him, open and inquisitive, and thanks to his complete mastery of his features his face took on an expression of mild, indulgent patience. He moved closer to the window. As though he wanted to steal radiance from outside and appear in an innocent light.

'We would like to talk to you about them,' Sejer said.

Axel noticed that Skarre was already busy taking notes.

'At some point during the night Jon got up and went outside,' Sejer said. 'He sneaked out of the cabin while you and Reilly were asleep. You heard nothing, so we don't know what time that was.'

Axel had found a comfortable position leaning against the wall.

'If we presume that he left with the intention of drowning himself in the lake,' Sejer went on, 'there are several things which are hard to understand.'

It grew silent in Axel's living room. He rarely found himself with nothing to say and he realised that the very silence itself was revealing.

'Jon was wearing very warm clothing,' Sejer said. 'If I hadn't known better, I would have assumed he was dressed for a walk in the forest.'

Axel smiled a glum smile.

'Surely it's not very odd,' he declared, 'that he put on a jacket. It was just out of habit. Because he was going outside.'

'He had buttoned all the buttons,' Sejer said. 'He laced up his boots and tied a double knot.'

Skarre looked up from his notepad. It was already covered with writing.

'Jon was very neat,' Axel said. 'In absolutely every situation. Take the laces. We used to tease him about them. He always tied a double knot. In winter, when we were kids, we had to pour warm water on those knots to untie them.'

He turned away for a moment. He could see the river from the window and while no help could be found there, he needed some breathing space. The way they obsessed about minor things aggravated him, as though it was he who had driven Jon over the edge or as if somehow he could explain to them how suicidal people behave during their final hour.

'I don't know,' he said. 'I'm not an expert. Perhaps he was unable to go to sleep and he might just have wanted to go for a walk initially, that was why he got dressed properly. And then something overwhelmed him, something broke him. Some sort of despondency or a melancholy which got too much for him. After all, he did suffer from anxiety.'

'Yes,' Sejer said, 'that is a possibility. That something overcame him later and it all happened very quickly. First he gets dressed with military precision and then he jumps off a cliff.'

Axel was not sure what Sejer was thinking. His lined face did not reveal much, apart from scepticism.

Skarre looked up from his notepad. 'There's another detail which baffles us,' he said. 'I'm talking about the fact that Jon could not swim. But we found him quite far out. One hundred metres from shore, to be precise. How did he get that far?'

Axel was slightly taken aback.

'I imagine that he drifted for a while,' he said. 'I don't know.'

'There's no current in that lake,' Skarre said.

'I don't think it's up to me to explain this,' Axel said, 'as you are well aware. I work in advertising. I don't know about such things.'

'Right,' Sejer said. 'That's our job. Isn't it, Skarre?'

'It is our job,' Skarre agreed.

Sejer retrieved something from his inside pocket and Axel recognised Jon's mobile. Axel knew that Jon had a photo of a small white dog on the display.

'We've obviously got the phone records,' Sejer explained. He started pressing the keys.

'Sent box,' he said. 'Friday 13th September, text sent to Molly Gram, just before ten o'clock in the evening. Molly was Jon's girlfriend at Ladegården,' he added. 'Did you know that he had a girlfriend?'

Axel could feel his composure trickle away.

'"Hi Molly. Trying to cope up here in the cabin. My anxiety seems to get worse when I'm away from the hospital. Hope I make it. Looking forward to seeing you on Sunday. Love, Jon."'

Sejer returned the mobile to his inside pocket.

'This text wasn't sent by someone planning to kill himself,' he stated.

'Jon might not have been thinking about it when he sent the message,' Axel said. 'Something must have happened in the course of the night.'

'Did he feel threatened?'

'By us, you mean?' Axel said. 'We're his best friends.'

'He was looking forward to Sunday,' Skarre said. 'But he never came back to Ladegården. He didn't make it. What do you think happened to him?'

'Jon was very volatile,' Axel explained. 'His mood changed from one hour to the next, up and down, like a roller coaster. The guy was worn out. You won't be able to find a logical explanation for what happened.'

Sejer and Skarre exchanged looks. Simultaneously they got up from the sofa and prepared to leave.

CHAPTER 7

Reilly was standing in the doorway holding the kitten.

His pale skin was covered with thin, red claw marks.

'Come on,' Axel said. 'We need to go and see Ingerid.'

'Do we have to?'

'Yes, we do. We can't put it off any longer, she's expecting us. She probably has a lot of questions, so we have to make up something which sounds plausible. About that evening. What Jon said and did, how he was, all the little details that she'll want to know. How are you?' he asked. 'You're not high, I hope?'

Reilly grunted a reply. He went back inside the flat, a tiny studio on the fourth floor. His bed was unmade.

'I need to feed the kitten first,' he said.

Axel followed. He slammed the door shut.

'Forget about the kitten,' he said. 'Have you gone mad? We need to leave now. The situation is getting a bit tense,' he added. 'The police are all over this with a diligence I've never seen before. You would think it was our fault Jon ended up in the lake.'

'Perhaps it was,' Reilly said.

He went over to the kitchen counter. He filled the kitten's bowl with fresh water and opened a tin of cat food. He mashed the food, which consisted of chunks of meat in gravy, with a fork until it turned into a smooth grey and brown mush. He carried out these simple tasks with great care and he did not permit Axel to interrupt him.

'Now don't pee on the carpet,' he told the kitten. 'Do your business in the litter tray.'

'Snap out of it,' Axel said. 'We need to go.'

Reilly leaned against the kitchen counter. His long hair was unwashed and hung in thin strands over his shoulders.

'I don't know what to say,' he said. 'You go on your own. With your big mouth you can do the talking for both of us.'

Axel grunted irritably.

'I can't take care of everything,' he said. 'I'm exhausted. Now get a grip.'

Reilly put on his long coat. He threw a last, worried glance at the kitten and followed Axel. The old stairs creaked as they walked down to the ground floor. Shortly afterwards they were driving through the town in Axel's Mercedes, scarab green with gorgeous white leather seats. As always it was newly washed and polished. Reilly watched the world through its windows and the people they passed. We're not like them, he thought, we lack decency. We lack a normal sense of justice.

He pondered these things for a while.

'What do you think it is about us?' he asked.

'What do you mean?' Axel said.

'I mean, that we did what we did. Does it mean that we're not quite right?'

'What are you on about now?' Axel asked.

'Well, you know, there's something called emotional intelligence,' Reilly elaborated. 'Empathy. Understanding. Conscience. Remorse. The ability to comprehend the consequences of your actions. Some people have low emotional intelligence.'

This caused Axel to brake so abruptly that the tyres screeched. He pulled over and stopped the car.

'Are you saying that there is something wrong with me?' he said. 'That I don't have feelings like other people? Are you saying that I'm not grieving? That I have low emotional intelligence just because Jon threw himself into the lake?'

Reilly retreated slightly. 'To be honest, I'm not really sure,' he said.

'There is nothing wrong with my emotional intelligence,' Axel snapped. 'Jesus, what an idea! You've got to quit that reading of yours, it's doing your head in.'

'But most people would not have acted the way we did,' he wailed.

Axel checked his mirror and pulled out into the road again.

'Most people don't end up in that kind of situation,' he said, 'and I won't listen to any more talk like that.'

'But I've got such a bad conscience.'

'I don't understand this fuss about conscience,' Axel said. 'It's not like you can take a clear conscience with you to your grave.'

Reilly felt like saying something about conscience. It stays behind after we die, he thought, like light or like shadow. And those who come after us grow up in that shadow. The sins of the fathers, he mused. But Axel would not understand these things. Axel would ask if he was thinking of getting married or having kids since he was going on about future generations. No one will want a scruffy old hippie like you, he would say. And he might be right.

'Our society is based on important values,' Reilly said out loud. He held up three fingers. 'The rule of law, truth and justice. But we've made our own rules.'

'There isn't one set of rules which apply universally,' Axel declared. 'You understand that, don't you? Such notions depend on culture. And history. And religion. And, not least, circumstances. By the way, why are you reading the Koran?'

'It's Nader from work,' Reilly said. 'Nader talks about the Koran the whole time. The most beautiful message about peace in the world.'

'If you're feeling that much guilt,' Axel said, 'then throw away the Koran and become a Catholic.'

Ingerid Moreno came to the door immediately to greet them. She no longer looked like the Ingerid they knew. Despair controlled her body like pain in every joint, and she moved around like an old woman. Axel got a cautious hug, but she was more reserved towards Reilly. As per usual Axel was sincere in his compassion. Why is that man not on the stage? Reilly thought, he's a born actor. But perhaps life itself was his stage and everyone he met his devoted audience. Ingerid invited them in. Reilly watched her large, heavy breasts undulate beneath her blouse. Jon used to lie at those breasts, Reilly thought, it must have been a good place to be. Jon did not take after his mother, he thought next. Jon was thin and slight, while Ingerid was plump and broad-shouldered. But the Italian Moreno, who was Jon's father, had been slight, too, he recalled. A small, slender guy who had left them when Jon was a little boy.

'I know he found things difficult,' Ingerid said. 'Young people often do. But he was getting help.'

She looked at them across the table.

'What do you think?' she asked. 'Tell me what you think. You were with him that last evening.'

Reilly was unable to utter a single word, but Axel spoke freely, as he always did.

'I suppose he was a bit gloomy,' he said, 'a little low. He did not say much, you know what he was like. He didn't drink much either, Jon was quite restrained like that. He didn't do much crazy stuff, you need to know that, Ingerid.'

He opened his arms helplessly.

'Anxiety is impossible,' he said. 'An enemy you can't see or hear.'

Ingerid Moreno started wringing her hands in her lap.

'But when did it start?' she asked. 'Did you notice when he first started to feel anxious? Did he talk about it? Was it last winter?'

Axel and Reilly exchanged glances.

'Did something happen? I've tried thinking back,' she said, 'but I can't put my finger on anything. Could it have been to do with a girl? Girlfriend trouble can get very bad, I know all about that, I was married to an Italian.'

Axel smiled a kind smile.

'Jon wasn't involved with girls,' he said. 'Jon was very shy, you know that. If a girl even so much as looked at him, his ears would go bright red.'

'Yes,' Ingerid remembered. 'His ears used to go very red.'

She gave them a look of resignation.

'When the hospital told me he was going on this trip, I was very sceptical. But when they explained he was going with you two, I didn't mind. Then I knew he would be in safe hands.'

Reilly felt a lump in his throat. He thought about their safe hands which had not managed to save Jon. His eyes sought the window; they lingered on a treetop where a crow made a branch sway, slowly, like a child on a swing.

'Shy or not,' Ingerid said, 'he did have a friend at Ladegården. Her name is Molly and she was in the same ward. Jon doesn't get close to people very easily so it made me happy. Because it's so important to have friends, and of course, a girlfriend. I had hoped that Molly might become his girlfriend. That he would finally have had someone to confide in.'

Her lower lip started to quiver.

'I know he was holding something back,' she hiccuped. 'Mothers always know. But whenever I asked, he would draw back. It must have been something serious since he was too scared to tell me. That's what I thought. Something really serious.'

At this point Axel and Reilly both chose to nod emphatically.

'His funeral is next Friday,' Ingerid said. 'At one o'clock. The vicar is coming tomorrow. I hope he is a considerate man and that he can find something to say, something meaningful. Please would you help me choose some music?' she asked. 'What did Jon like to listen to? Please tell me.'

'Madrugada,' Axel said.

'Madrugada, definitely,' Reilly said. 'Jon wouldn't have settled for anything less.'

'I see. Is that a band?'

'Yes. Jon liked Madrugada more than anything else. We can sort that out for you. We'll find something suitable.'

'We can't have rock music in a church,' she said.

'We'll pick something quiet,' Axel said. 'Trust us.'

'"Highway of Light,"' Reilly suggested.

'Yes, "Highway of Light", definitely,' Axel agreed. 'It will raise the roof of the church. It is grand and symphonic. It always used to send shivers down Jon's spine when he listened to it.'

'Thank you,' she said. 'You're so kind.'

She leaned forward across the table as if to crawl over to them.

'I wish he had left behind a letter,' she said. 'A last message. I have spoken to Hanna Wigert. She said he might have been struck by an acute psychosis, but we'll never know for sure.'

She wrung her hands on the table. Reilly grew scared that the joints of her fingers would snap.

'And then I need to talk to Molly. If she wants to see me. And his things need to be collected. I'm dreading it. Entering the room where he slept, taking his toothbrush out of the glass. His clothes and everything.'

'Let us do that, please,' Axel said. 'Then you won't have to.'

Again she smiled with gratitude.

'Thank you,' she whispered. 'You're so kind. Thank you for everything you have been for Jon, you meant so much to him. I'll never forget you two.'

She clasped their hands on the table.

'And now there's something I need to tell you,' she said.

She looked earnestly at them both.

'What happened must be difficult for you and perhaps you feel responsible, but you're not. I don't blame you for anything. Promise me, please, that you will put this behind you and move on.'

CHAPTER 8

Ladegården Psychiatric Hospital was a yellow, three-storey building set in an attractive park with sculptures and fountains. A network of paths bordered by flowers and bushes criss-crossed the grounds. Axel stopped the Mercedes in the visitors' car park and for a while they sat watching the yellow façade. Jon had slept behind one of the arched windows.

'His room was on the first floor,' Axel said.

Reilly started counting. 'It's up there,' he said, pointing. 'Fourth window from the left.'

Axel stuck a Marlboro in his mouth and Reilly opened the car window. He did not want to go inside, did not want see Jon's room or his things. However, they had promised Ingerid Moreno they would take care of it. Axel finished his cigarette. They went to reception and explained why they had come.

'We would like to talk to Hanna Wigert,' Axel said. 'We're here to collect Jon Moreno's belongings.'

Reilly had imagined Hanna Wigert to be a big, sturdy woman. There was something about her name that proclaimed a full bust and broad shoulders. However, Hanna Wigert was small and composed with an impressive mane of red, curly hair. Reilly was aware that she was judging them. It appeared she was drawing some swift conclusions.

'So,' she said gravely. 'You wanted Jon's things?'

Axel nodded. He was wearing his wistful smile.

'I've been expecting you,' she said. 'Ingerid Moreno called.'

She studied them for several long seconds with a sharpness which made Reilly say a silent prayer. He had never felt so scrutinised. I need a fix, he thought.

She turned on her heel and walked off in white strappy shoes, noiseless against the linoleum floor. They followed her up a broad staircase where every step was edged with brass. It smelled as though someone had just washed it. Lemon, Reilly thought, or apple. Then they went down a long corridor until they reached a door. She opened it, and they looked inside. The room was reminiscent of a cell. The bed was stripped of linen and someone had taken Jon's clothes out of the wardrobe and dumped them on the mattress. A pair of trousers here, a sock and a jumper there. The pile of clothes made Reilly imagine that Jon had fallen apart like a doll and that he could not be put back together again. The mattress repelled him. It had blue and white stripes and was covered with a kind of plastic sheet, through which he could detect some stains.

'There's not much,' Hanna Wigert said. 'Just some clothes. And his stereo and CDs. I'll get you some boxes.'

Reilly was restless. He paced up and down the floor, went over to the window and looked out at the park, at the paths and the fountains.

'I feel like an intruder,' he said. 'This is Jon's room. We've got no right to be here.'

'Let's just get it over with,' Axel said.

Reilly went to the bed and held a knitted jumper to his face. It was blue with a darker pattern across the chest. Suddenly he was surrounded by Jon. He inhaled the smell and his throat closed instantly as though a stick had been pushed down it.

'We need to fold them carefully,' Axel said, 'so Ingerid can see that we've made an effort. Don't just stand there. Procrastinating will only make it worse.'

Reilly was still pressing the jumper to his face. It was as if Jon were very close and wanted to tell him something. Bring me back, the voice said, I don't want to be alone here in the dark.

'Now get a move on,' Axel ordered him.

Hanna Wigert returned with the boxes. She put them down on the floor and placed her hands on her hips.

41

'If you understand anything about what's happened, I expect you to tell me,' she said.

Reilly let go of the jumper. Axel pulled the boxes towards him. It said Evergood on one and Delikat on the other.

'It came as a shock,' he said. 'But then again, he was ill,' he added.

'Ill,' Hanna Wigert echoed. 'Not suicidal.'

Axel picked up a pair of trousers. Hanna Wigert did not take her eyes off him. There was something ominous about her disapproving look and her wild red hair.

'If you think that we bear some responsibility for this, then you're probably right,' Axel said. 'We should have seen that something was up, we should have taken more care. But we don't have your experience, we're just ordinary people.'

His words silenced her. She left, closing the door behind her, and Jon's room fell quiet.

'She's one angry woman,' Axel said. 'She practically had steam coming out of her ears. I thought she would blow her top.'

'Jon liked her very much,' Reilly said.

'Jon was desperate,' Axel said. 'He liked anyone who was nice to him.'

That was when Reilly snapped. He grabbed hold of Axel and shook him.

'You're a prick,' he said, 'and you'll shut up now! Jon was worth much more than you!'

Axel grunted by way of reply. They packed Jon's belongings in silence: jumpers, trousers, underwear, CDs and a couple of books, socks. Axel thought they could pair the socks at random, but Reilly protested.

'Jon was very neat,' he said.

When everything was packed up, they surveyed the bare room.

'Look at the mirror,' Reilly said. 'It's plastic.'

'This is a desolate place,' Axel said. 'How do people stand it?'

'They have no choice,' Reilly argued.

They carried Jon's possessions to reception. Axel went down the stairs first. Reilly followed him, a little anxious about tripping in his long coat. He was carrying the heaviest box with books and CDs. Hanna Wigert was waiting for them. She gave them another long, critical look.

'There was just one more thing,' Axel said. He put the box on the floor. 'Could we meet Molly, please?'

'Meet Molly?' she said.

'After all, they were friends,' Axel said. 'Jon spoke so much about her and she would probably like to go to his funeral. It's on Friday. One o'clock. I thought we could have a little chat.'

Hanna Wigert frowned.

'Molly has enough on her plate as it is,' she said.

'I'll understand if she says no,' Axel said, 'but please would you give her the choice? It's about Jon. She'll probably want to know.'

Hanna Wigert looked defeated.

'I don't even know where she is.'

'But you could check her room, please?' Axel asked. 'We understand that you have to protect your patients, but some decisions they have to make for themselves.'

Axel's impertinence made Hanna Wigert feel dizzy. She gestured towards a small waiting room and went to find Molly Gram, walking off this time with a touch of indignation so that her otherwise noiseless shoes could be heard against the floor. Axel and Reilly sat looking out of the large windows. The sound of a lawnmower cut through the silence.

'What do you want with her?' Reilly whispered.

'I just need to check something,' Axel said. 'Find out if she knows anything.'

Reilly shook his head, despairing. 'And if she knows something, what are you going to do?'

Axel grabbed a magazine and started flicking through it.

'We need to know where we stand,' he said. 'I need to be in control. I'll be able to tell immediately if she knows something.'

Reilly stuffed his big hands in his coat pockets.

'If Jon confided in Molly, there's sod all we can do about it. Or what did you have in mind?'

Axel did not reply. They listened towards the corridor. The big building was strangely quiet; no shouting, no laughter, no footsteps. But they could hear a distant drone as from a big engine far away, or perhaps it was located underneath them, in the basement.

A young woman entered the room. The light from one of the tall windows glowed behind her. She was slender as a reed, with wispy blonde hair and harshly made up eyes. She wore a ballerina's tutu with tights underneath and ballet pumps on her feet. In her arms she was cradling a small white dog.

Good heavens, Reilly thought. Molly Gram is an angel.

She looked at them with black eyes. Suddenly the dog freed itself, leapt down to the floor and ran to greet Axel. However, Axel ignored the small, shaggy animal, and after several failed attempts at getting his attention, it ran over to Reilly instead. Here it received a warmer welcome. Reilly stroked its head and the dog began nipping at the legs of his corduroy trousers. Reilly waited patiently. He could not make himself shoo it away and he did not move his leg. He saw that the dog had got its teeth into a torn flap of worn fabric and was pulling at it. After a while it started growling as though it were playing with another dog and Reilly decided to withdraw his foot. No good. The dog was fixed to his trouser leg. It had no intention of giving up its prey, even if it was only a scrap of corduroy. He looked towards Molly for help.

'Melis,' she said. 'Drop it.'

The command was barely audible, but the dog instantly let go, spun around and ran back to her.

Axel stepped forward to greet her.

'My name's Axel,' he said, 'and the giant here is Philip Reilly. It's kind of you to see us, we really appreciate it. We're friends of Jon.'

He took both of her hands in his and Reilly knew that Axel's hands were warm, and that the warmth would spread to her whole

44

body. You might even think he had hands like a healer. Reilly had seen many girls go weak at the knees, but Axel Frimann had no effect on Molly. She stood very still and looked at him with her black eyes.

'We thought you might want to go to the funeral,' Axel said. 'It's on Friday, in Brodal Church. One o'clock.'

She measured him from his head down to his Italian leather shoes.

'We used to walk together,' she said. 'In the evening. After dinner.'

'Where did you go?' Axel asked. 'Tell us, please.'

'Through the park,' she said, 'and down the path. It runs in a figure of eight through the forest and it's just the right distance. It took us an hour. And we would stop on the way back and drink water from the fish fountain up there. There is a carp that spews water.'

Axel smiled. 'If you want to go to the funeral, we could come and pick you up,' he offered.

'I'll be getting a lift with Hanna,' she said.

A pause followed.

She looked as if she was about to leave.

'Melis!' she called out. 'Come here.'

'Jon was really into you,' Axel said.

She took one step forward.

'What happened?' she asked.

'At the cabin, you mean?'

'Yes.'

'We don't know,' Axel said. 'He went out during the night while we were sleeping. He was gone when we got up.'

She shook her head.

'No,' she said. 'We had an agreement. Jon would not have broken our agreement.'

'Everybody does sooner or later,' Axel said. 'If they don't, they're not human. Please don't judge Jon even though he might have disappointed you.'

She fixed her kohl-black eyes on him again.

'Judge Jon? Are you even listening to me?'

She headed for the door. Her narrow back disappeared. Melis ran after her.

The men left. They turned around and looked back at the yellow façade. Reilly got the feeling that Molly was watching them from a window.

'That girl's still having toddler tantrums,' Axel said. 'You know the way they stamp their feet.'

'She's ill,' Reilly reminded him.

'It's not that she's ill,' Axel said. 'More that she's a wildcat. If you want to catch one of those, you need to wear protective gloves.'

CHAPTER 9

In her office Hanna Wigert had a blue sofa with a high back. It was a two-seater and had come from her childhood home in Kragerø. When she was a little girl she used to jump up and down on it. She had climbed its tall back and watched the shimmering sea through the windows. Sometimes, in the evenings, she had fallen asleep on it and her father had carried her off to bed without her noticing. When her parents had died she had collected the sofa and put it in her office. It reminded her of goodness. Not everyone had grown up in such fortunate circumstances, and some of those people came to this office. Now the sofa was covered with rag dolls and cuddly toys. They were piled in a big heap, and they took up a lot of room.

She shook Sejer's hand and asked him to sit down. He moved dolls and animals and she noticed that he handled them with the utmost care. They were not tossed aside, but were gently placed against the armrests of the sofa.

'What do you want to know?' Hanna Wigert asked.

Sejer moved a sheep with a curly fleece.

'What did you think when you heard about Jon's suicide?' he said.

'I was surprised,' she said.

'Why?'

She considered this for a long time. Her hair, it struck him, looked like wool. Like the sheep's.

'Because it was unexpected,' she said. 'Everyone gives off light. You can see it in their eyes or their bodies or in the way they move. You can tell that something drives them. It's a form of energy. Jon Moreno's light was still safe and sound.'

His light was safe and sound, Sejer thought. What a lovely way of putting it.

'He was getting help,' she said, 'and he was grateful for that. He kept so much deep inside him, but he was opening up. To some extent it's also a matter of intuition,' she said. 'I've been here a long time. I've seen many fall by the wayside. But when you called and told me that Jon was dead, I nearly fell off my chair. That shouldn't happen to a psychiatrist.'

Sejer held up one of the rag dolls. It had short yellow hair made from yarn, blue eyes and it wore a red dress decorated with white beads.

'Did he ever talk about death?'

'He never mentioned death at all,' Hanna Wigert said. 'But that in itself isn't necessarily significant; suicide can happen without warning. Sometimes the strain builds and we don't notice. And then lightning strikes.'

Sejer looked at all the dolls that surrounded him.

'What are they for?' he asked.

'Oh,' she said. 'They're here to make it cosy. And they serve a practical purpose, too. Opening up and exposing yourself isn't easy. Your hands have nothing to do. So I give the patients something to handle.'

Sejer looked at the rag doll in his lap.

'They pick very different ones,' she said. 'Some are attracted to one in particular, which they always go to fetch when they come here. Others take a new one every time. Others think the whole thing is ridiculous. The doll in your lap is called Lady Di.'

'They've got names?'

'Nearly all of them.'

Sejer put down Lady Di and picked up a pink velvet pig with a curly tail.

'Let me guess,' he said. 'Girls pick this one.'

'Yes,' Hanna Wigert smiled. 'The pig.'

'What did Jon Moreno do?'

She got up from her chair, dug through the pile and pulled out a rag doll with short black hair.

'He used to hold this one,' she said. 'It's a boy rag doll and Jon spotted it immediately.'

She held it up to him. It was obviously made by someone who knew their craft. Its eyes and brows were neatly embroidered with shiny black thread. Its hair was short and stuck out, and the doll was wearing blue denim dungarees.

'Who makes them?' Sejer asked.

'The patients,' Hanna Wigert said. 'In the workshop. New ones arrive every year and some take their favourite dolls home. Others want to leave something behind when they go, so that we will remember them. The teddy is called Barney,' she said, 'and the one with the gap between its teeth is called Kurt.'

'What about Jon's doll? Does it have a name?'

'It's called Kim.'

'Kim. Why is that?'

'He told me it reminded him of someone he met once. He wouldn't say anything more and I don't know if it was significant, but the doll is called Kim.'

Sejer squeezed the doll's tummy as though he expected it to squeak.

'Some people have a negative reaction,' Hanna Wigert said. 'They think my office is childish. But in time they get used to the rag dolls. It's important to be a little childish,' she added and flashed a smile at the inspector. He's quite attractive, she thought, and she enjoyed playing a bit on her femininity, of which she had plenty when it suited her.

Sejer examined Kim the rag doll with renewed interest. It was roughly thirty centimetres long, made from golden brown canvas and wore tiny socks on its feet.

'There's something I need to tell you,' Hanna Wigert said. 'Jon didn't want to go on the trip to the cabin.'

'Did he say as much?'

She picked up a doll from the pile. Now she needed something to fidget with.

'He practically begged me not to make him go. But I was so

keen to get him out among other people, that I talked him into it. I explained it was vital to keep in touch with the world outside. And he was going with his friends. They would take good care of him. I didn't take my cue from him. That was unforgivable, and it will haunt me for the rest of my life.'

She slumped a little in her chair. She raised a hand to her eyes.

'Did he say why he didn't want to go?'

'I tried to press him, but he was evasive. And I'm breaking my duty of confidentiality here, but you represent an authority which allows me to do so,' she said. 'Jon suffered badly from anxiety. He believed that his anxiety would worsen if he left the ward, that it would overcome him in the forest. And it clearly did.'

'And yet you're surprised at what happened,' he said. 'What makes someone commits suicide out of the blue?'

She tossed her doll back on the sofa.

'It's called a psychological accident,' she said. 'Several factors present themselves simultaneously and lead to a fatal outcome.'

'Such as?'

She thought again.

'I'm trying to find a story,' she said, 'which can illustrate what I mean. I should have quite a few to choose from because I've seen this before. Oh, yes, I recall a story from Sweden that's a good example.'

She leaned forward eagerly.

'A man spends the weekend at a cabin with some friends,' she began. 'They go elk hunting. After a long time he returns home to his wife with fresh elk meat. Monday morning he gets into his car and drives to work. He has a well-paid job with a renowned firm. Then his boss comes into his office and tells him that the company has to cut costs, and that sadly he will have to let him go. In a few seconds he loses everything. His financial independence, his sense of belonging and his status. He gets into his car to drive home, overwhelmed by despondency. His entire world has collapsed. He pulls over at a bus stop, where he sits in despair.

Then he remembers that his rifle is still in the boot of his car after the hunting trip. He fetches the weapon, loads it and shoots himself through the head.'

Sejer listened to her story.

'He didn't have time to think of another solution,' he said.

'Precisely,' Hanna Wigert said. 'Two things occured simultaneously. A crisis and access to a weapon.'

'What do you think might have happened to Jon?'

'I don't know. I don't understand it. According to his mother he started getting ill last winter. Up until then he was well-adjusted, but very sensitive. In some way he was predisposed, of course, but we are not aware of any inherited tendencies, and he never hinted at an experience or a trauma which might explain it.'

'Did he confide in any of the patients?'

'He became friends with one of the girls here. She doesn't understand it either.'

She scrutinised him.

'Why are you here?' she asked.

'It's pure routine in cases like this one . . .'

'In case he didn't take his own life,' she completed the sentence for him. 'But met his death in some other way?'

'Yes,' Sejer conceded. 'I suppose you're right.'

'What have you found out?'

Sejer hesitated.

'I can't discuss that,' he said.

'But you've found something, haven't you?'

'Let me put it this way,' Sejer said. 'There are a couple of things that disturb us. Details which we don't understand.'

Hanna Wigert stared down at her lap. She reminded him of a defiant little girl.

'He couldn't swim,' she said.

'We know,' Sejer said.

'Those two friends of his,' she continued. 'They had a great deal of power over him.'

'Where are you going with this?'

She retreated as though she was on shaky ground, and he did not get a reply.

He was still holding Kim in his lap. He pinched the coarse yarn hair and carefully tugged at the tiny white socks. They reminded him of the rubber caps you put on your fingertips when you want to leaf through a stack of papers. Reacting to an impulse, which he could not account for, a small request escaped him.

'Please may I take this with me?'

'The doll?'

'I want to keep it in my office.'

'But what do you want with it?'

'It's a link to Jon,' he said. 'And after all, it's important to be a little childish.'

Afterwards he spoke to Molly Gram.

She refused to come downstairs, but she had said he could go to her room. When he entered, she was sitting on her bed with the white dog on her lap. It was a terrier, he noticed. It pricked up its ears. Sejer held out his hand, but she did not take it. The dog, however, expressed interest: it licked and sniffed it. He pulled out a chair and sat down by her bed.

'You can ask your questions now,' she said.

Sejer studied the sullen young woman with paternal interest. Her hair was in a total mess, dry and soft like cotton grass. Underneath the black make-up she was sweet, but she wanted to come across as something else; the make-up served almost as a declaration of war. She was fierce, bitter and dismissive, and it was not up to him to decide if she had good cause to be. For a while he pondered how to approach her. Her body might be small and fragile, he thought, but she had an old head on those young shoulders.

'There's a game I like to play when I meet new people,' he said.

She rolled her eyes. She stroked Melis across his back.

'I give them a place in the animal kingdom,' Sejer said. 'According to their attributes. And their appearance.'

She continued to caress the dog with her fingers as thin as noodles, and he could see that she was listening.

'I decide very quickly,' Sejer said, 'and if an animal doesn't spring to mind, then I'll never find out who they are. Some are impossible to categorise or too vague, while others are blatantly obvious.'

Long pause. She had hunched her shoulders, and he noticed a wasp tattoo on her white neck.

'When I saw you, I made up my mind almost immediately,' he said. 'It took me seconds.'

She stopped caressing Melis. Her eye make-up was so dark that it looked like a mask, but this time she was watching him intently.

'You're a racoon,' Sejer said.

She pulled a face. She needed time to decide what she thought about the comparison, but before she had time to feel anything at all, she was interrupted.

'They're fast and smart and cheeky,' Sejer said, 'and they steal food from others. They're rogues, and they get everywhere. And they're beautiful, of course.'

She might be an old soul, but Molly managed a smile. At least Sejer thought he saw something flicker across her face.

'Do you want me to go on?' he said. 'Do you want me to tell you more about the racoon?'

She deigned to shrug, which he took to mean that he could do whatever he wanted.

'Racoons are very popular,' he said. 'Do you know why?'

She did not reply.

'Molly,' he said. 'Can you imagine why everyone wants a racoon?'

'No,' she mumbled.

'Well, this might sound a little brutal,' he smiled, 'but you're no sissy. Their meat is very tasty and their fur is the loveliest in the world. And they happen to thrive in captivity,' he added. He let his eyes flash around her room.

'You can put them in cages and they won't lose their integrity.'

'They came to fetch Jon's things,' she said. 'Those two friends of his.'

Sejer pricked up his ears.

'Go on.'

She held Melis up to her face. 'I can play this game too, and I got Axel's number at once.'

'He's no pussycat,' Sejer said. 'We agree on that, don't we?'

'He's a snake,' she said. 'He slithers around.'

'And Reilly?' Sejer asked.

She pondered this.

'He's a lizard,' she declared. 'They aren't easy on the eye, but they're better than their reputation. The bigger ones can be dangerous to humans and the smaller ones can make good pets. You never know with lizards. Perhaps they become what you make them.'

She put Melis down on the bed, pinched a corner of the duvet and started twisting it.

'You can ask your questions now,' she said again.

Sejer looked at the racoon on the bed. She was wearing a red minidress and black knee-high socks.

'You were the last person to talk to Jon before he got into the car. What did you talk about?'

She kept picking at the duvet.

'That will remain between Jon and me,' she said.

'But can you tell me anything about his state of mind?'

'State of mind? He was happy.'

'Really?' Sejer said. 'He was happy? I'm sorry. I'm a bit taken aback. It was my impression that he didn't want to go on the trip at all. That he went along because the staff here thought it was important. But you're saying that he was happy?'

'He was happy.'

'He said so?'

'You can tell.'

'Tell me what you saw,' Sejer asked.

'He started running,' she explained. 'The car pulled up in front of the building and Jon started running.'

Sejer waited but nothing more followed.

'And that means that he was happy?'

She looked up.

'No one runs here at Ladegården,' she sighed. 'We're depressed, we drag ourselves around. Surely you can understand that.'

Sejer smiled and shook his head.

'So what did you say to him?' he asked. 'What made him run so fast?'

She grew shy and looked away.

'That will remain between Jon and me,' she said. 'But let me put it this way, we were making plans.'

'For the future, you mean?'

She nodded. Again she held Melis up to her face.

'Jon spent the night in the company of those two reptiles,' she said, 'and I don't know what happened. But we had plans.'

CHAPTER 10

Reilly put some fine sand in a turquoise plastic box and placed it below the kitchen window. The kitten instantly knew that it was meant to do its business there. At night the kitten slept in Reilly's bed, curled up at his throat, and when it purred it felt like humming against his vocal cords. When Reilly wandered around his flat, it followed him faithfully. You think you're a puppy, don't you, though cats are supposed to be independent, didn't you know that? But the kitten was not independent. It stuck to him like a limpet. Every time Reilly let himself fall into a chair to get high or to read the Koran it would claw at his corduroy trousers to be allowed up. In the morning when he had to go to work, it looked after him with lost eyes which were still blue. Reilly worked as a porter at the Central Hospital. He thought constantly about the kitten while he rolled beds down the corridors. He rolled children to the playroom, he rolled people in for surgery, he rolled the deceased down to the mortuary in the basement. He was in the habit of whistling quietly as he walked. And all the while he thought about the kitten.

Over the years, Reilly had started making mistakes, and sometimes the beds had ended up in the wrong place. He had been given a warning and he pulled himself together after that. God forbid that I roll someone who is still breathing down to the mortuary, he thought.

Reilly was going through his wardrobe looking for some smart clothes to wear for Jon's funeral, but he had never owned nice clothes. Everything he had was worn and faded and almost none of it was clean. Most of what he found looked like rags, and he threw them in a pile on the floor. The kitten leapt on top of it to play. Having searched carefully for a long time, he found a high-necked jumper and a pair of khaki combat trousers with numerous pockets. The trousers were creased and it worried him. Yet he felt reasonably pleased, though other thoughts soon dragged him down. The kitten watched him while he got dressed and when he had finished, he took out the Koran.

What is the Day of Noise and Clamour? And what will explain to thee what the Day of Noise and Clamour is? It is a Day whereon men will be like moths scattered about, and the mountains will be like carded wool. Then, he whose balance of good deeds will be found heavy, will be in a life of good pleasure and satisfaction. But he whose balance of good deeds will be found light will have his home in a bottomless Pit. And what will explain to thee what this is? It is a Fire blazing fiercely!

He put the book away. He had studied the Koran extensively, but he did not believe in God. He just liked to pretend that a higher power existed. Now he had read that a punishment awaited him for everything he had done. It was a pit of burning fire. He did not believe in that either and that was a relief, but he told himself that he was atoning in his own way by repeatedly exposing himself to the violent threats in the Koran.

Axel picked him up in the Mercedes.

He was wearing a well-cut suit and a plum-coloured shirt, and he looked Reilly up and down.

'We're saying goodbye to Jon,' he said. 'And you look like a tramp.'

Reilly was aghast. He did not think the jumper was as bad as that, and the khaki trousers were his best pair.

'Jon would not have cared about a few creases,' he muttered.

He trudged down the stairs after Axel and got into the car. From the corner of his eye he studied Axel's suit. It was charcoal with thin lapels and he also wore a long coat.

'You could have done something with your hair,' Axel continued. 'It's just hanging there.'

He leaned forward to see what Reilly was wearing on his feet.

'You haven't even got laces in your shoes,' he pointed out. 'Why not?'

'They snapped,' Reilly said. He fumbled with the seat belt.

'It's about time you took a good look at yourself in the mirror,' Axel said.

'I haven't got one,' Reilly said.

'You must have one in your bathroom?'

'It broke.'

'And how did you manage that?'

'I don't remember exactly. I must have been high. I don't have to account for every minute of the day,' he added, a little hurt because Axel was pinpointing his bad habits.

Nothing more was said. They drove on in silence and Reilly watched people through the windows of the car. Each and every one of them was going somewhere, yet it looked as if they were all lost. As if they did not know the streets and were complete strangers to the town.

'It would be very odd', he said out loud, 'if there's no purpose behind it all. Life. And us.'

'Don't start all that,' Axel said.

'But think about snowflakes,' Reilly said. 'And the Northern Lights.'

'They're beautiful,' Axel said, 'but they prove nothing.'

'So you think that beauty is completely random?' Reilly said. 'People who require proof of everything are impoverished,' he carried on. 'They're afraid to surrender to something. They're scared to lose control.'

'You're a dreamer,' Axel said. 'You'll never make anything of yourself.'

'You mean I'll never earn what you earn?'

'Correct,' Axel said.

'I was right,' Reilly replied. 'You're dirt poor.'

Again he stared out of the window at all the lost people.

'Do you think his dad will be there?' he said.

'Tony Moreno, you mean?'

'Yes.'

'No idea. They never had any contact. Perhaps he's got a new family. Perhaps Jon has a pile of siblings he never got to meet, a bunch of mini-Morenos running around in Naples.'

'What do you intend to say in the church?' Reilly asked.

'Just the usual,' Axel said. 'The stuff people want to hear.'

A dark, slender man sat in the front pew close to the wall, and though he was small, his white linen suit made him stand out. It was Tony Moreno, who had come all the way from Naples. He was huddled up on the pew as though he did not want to be seen, as though he did not want people to remember that he had left when Jon was little. The vicar had done his bit. He moved aside when Axel stepped up in his well-cut suit. In his hand he held a sheet of paper which quivered, but his voice was clear and sincere when he spoke.

'Jon,' he said. 'You were a unique person.'

A sigh rippled through the congregation. His voice carried beautifully through the church and he looked very handsome in his grey suit. He stood close to the coffin. It was made from mahogany, and an abundance of flowers covered the dark wood. He was obviously deeply moved. The fact that he had lied about some important details surrounding Jon's death did not strip him of the right to mourn, he believed, and it was good to feel a bit sentimental.

'You were intelligent, humble and compassionate,' he carried on. 'And you had a strong conscience, which reacted to the slightest thing. You were a better person than us. You cared about the weak, you felt the injustice of the world, and sometimes you allowed it to torment you. You were in the eye of the storm your whole life.'

At this point Axel looked up at the mourners and he saw that they were mesmerised. He could also see what they were thinking. That this Frimann, this friend of Jon's, was indeed a good-looking man, well-dressed, articulate, sincere. He granted Ingerid Moreno, who was sitting in the front pew, a sympathetic smile.

'You asked much of yourself and others,' he said. 'You were a good friend. You were honest, patient and extremely sensitive. Your sensitivity made it difficult for you to enjoy both the big and the little things in life. Eventually it got too much for you. While we were sleeping, you were swept away by your own black thoughts. We don't understand and we're completely at a loss. What was it we failed to see? What was it we did not understand?'

Axel turned to the coffin and bowed respectfully.

'As long as there is breath in us, we will remember the good times,' he said. 'Jon Moreno. We thank you.'

They carried Jon to his grave to the tune of Madrugada's 'Highway of Light'. Axel and Reilly walked at the front; behind them were Jon's cousin and the diminutive Tony Moreno in his white suit. At the back were two colleagues from Siba Computers. The six men struggled to find their rhythm, but after a clumsy start they managed to carry their burden with the speed and dignity that suited someone's final journey.

They came out into the blinding light. Reilly tried to adapt his pace. From time to time he would peek at Axel who was walking steadily on the left. Far away someone slammed a car door. They continued their slow progress. Reilly shifted his gaze from the vicar's cassock, which undulated in front of him, and he recognised Molly Gram. She was wearing a green dress and with her white hair she reminded him of a dandelion in seed. She was not with the other mourners. She stood to one side with Melis on her arm. Reilly could see the dog was struggling to be let loose. She must have left it in the car while they had been inside the church, he thought, and now that it was all over, she had gone to get it. It really was very shaggy. It reminded him of one of those mops you use to wash floors.

He stared ahead once more, at the vicar's back and rediscovered his rhythm. They did not have far to go now, he could see the black grave and the sight of it made him feel weak. For the second time he sensed movement and he realised Melis must have jumped down from Molly's arm. The terrier raced towards them and everything happened incredibly quickly. Overjoyed at seeing him again it latched on to Reilly's trouser leg with great determination. The terrier got hold of the cord running through the drawstring hem of his trouser leg. Reilly tried to shake his foot loose, but in the process he shifted the coffin's centre of gravity, and the broken rhythm spread to the other pall-bearers. Axel, on the left-hand side, got into trouble and the cousin and the two colleagues from Siba Computers shifted from foot to foot to maintain their balance. Tony Moreno ended up squatting. He squeezed the brass handle so hard his hand grew white from lack of circulation. A hush of fear went through the mourners. All six men staggered hopelessly back and forth as the little dog yanked and tugged at Reilly's trousers. The mourners at the rear stopped, some clasped their mouths and others clutched their chests. Molly started shouting and the coffin began to slide forwards. A violent struggle followed to keep it in position, but the disaster was inevitable. Jon's coffin sloped mercilessly towards the ground. A corner of it hit the slate-covered path with a crack. The flowers skidded off and arranged themselves in a heap at the feet of the vicar, a sea of roses, lilies and white ribbons. With love. From all of us.

Melis let go and rushed quick as lightning back into Molly's arms. The men lifted up the coffin again. One corner of it was damaged: the jagged wood glowed bright, but no one said a word. Later Reilly remembered that Tony Moreno made the sign of the cross.

The wake was held in the church hall.

Tony Moreno appeared in the doorway. He stared at the buzzing crowd, then hesitated before he turned around and left. People looked after him as he hurried off, a small man in a crumpled suit. Axel told funny stories, Ingerid cried, but she had to laugh, too, because he was a brilliant storyteller, and even better at making things up, Reilly thought. After all, he had played a part in most of the incidents Axel described and he barely recognised them. In Axel's embellished version everything was wilder and madder. It did Ingerid good to laugh, the colour returned to her cheeks. After they had been chatting for a while, she remembered something important. Her bag was on the floor, and now she dipped into it to show them something. Her hand brought out a book. Its cover was made from coarse red fabric.

'Look what Hanna Wigert gave to me,' she said. 'It was in a drawer in Jon's room. It's a diary. He wrote a diary all the time he was at Ladegården.'

Axel gave her a baffled look. Reilly felt a blow to his stomach. A diary. Bloody hell.

'Hanna wanted to give it to me personally,' Ingerid said.

Axel nodded. He was gripping the edge of the table. Ingerid put the book back in her bag and clicked it shut.

'I will copy Jon,' she said. 'I'll put it in my desk drawer. One day, when I'm feeling very brave, I'll read it. Jon may not have wanted me to – after all, a diary is a private thing – but I might find some answers.'

Axel finally leapt into action. You could see him preparing for an attack. He drew his chair closer, leaned forward over the table and placed a hand on her arm. It was golden against her white skin, a strong, tanned hand with clearly visible veins.

'Think twice before you read it,' he said. 'Perhaps there were things he wanted to spare you.'

She looked surprised. Her eyebrows shot up.

'What would they be?'

'Well,' Axel hesitated. 'Those confessions may not be intended for our eyes. For yours, I mean.'

'But he's my son,' she said, 'and now I've got nothing left. Only his thoughts in that diary and I so want them.'

Axel tightened his grip on her arm.

'But the things you write in a diary are the very things you want to keep secret,' he said.

Ingerid Moreno started to waver.

'I know that. But Jon took his own life. He left me all alone again. Who is going to bury me now, can you tell me that? Do you know what this means? I'll have to die among strangers. I'll forgive Jon, but only if he had good reason.'

'Well,' Axel nodded. 'As long as you're not disappointed. As long as it doesn't make matters worse.'

Ingerid Moreno freed her arm from Axel's grip.

'Jon would never disappoint me,' she said. 'I'm sure of that.'

Axel was always the driving force in our little engine, Philip Reilly mused. He was in charge of operations and maintenance. He got us out of every scrape. Whenever it started rattling in one place, he would be there in a split second and tighten a bolt.

Whenever they needed forgiveness for some boyish prank, he would charm people into submission, men and women alike. They had been able to get away with anything. Axel Frimann had his own light, an overwhelming aura of warmth, and when he looked at people, their sense of self-worth would instantly soar. Now he had lost his usual composure. Axel was normally a man of action. He could turn every situation to his own advantage. He had no time for people who surrendered to their fate. But now it appeared that Jon's innermost thoughts were to be found inside that diary, and he was no longer in control.

'You know what this means, don't you?'

'You leave Ingerid alone,' Reilly said.

Axel stopped pacing. What had Ingerid said? That she would do as Jon had done and put the diary in a drawer. And then, when she summoned up the courage one day, she would read it.

'There's a desk just inside the front door,' he said. 'I bet the diary is in one of the drawers.'

Reilly gave him a horrified look. The ideas taking shape in Axel's head were more than he could tolerate.

'We need that diary,' Axel said.

'And here I was thinking I was the crazy one,' Reilly said. 'It is completely out of the question and I sincerely hope that you understand that.'

'The diary is evidence.'

'That depends on what Jon wrote in it,' Reilly said. 'Don't underestimate him.'

Axel crossed to the open window. He stared out of it, both hands planted firmly on the windowsill. His muscles bulged under his shirt and Reilly was reminded of an ox in front of a closed gate.

'Deep down you're really very naive,' he said. 'You think we've got a chance to get away with it all, but we don't. And that might be just as well. I've always known that this day would come. But then again, I'm not the one worrying about a top job with Repeat.'

'No, you live in a hovel,' Axel said. 'And you've got a crap job.'

'I like my hovel. I like moving beds around.'

Over at the window Axel groaned loudly. His broad back was outlined by the light from outside.

'Do you know what occurred to me in the church today?' he asked. 'Jon wouldn't have made it anyway. Jon was constantly on edge, breathless, practically. You would have thought he had a heart defect.'

Reilly was pondering something else.

'What do you think it looks like inside his coffin?' he asked.

'What are you on about now?'

'It hit the ground. Jon must have skidded forwards. Perhaps he's squashed up in a corner.'

'There's no room for movement inside a coffin,' Axel said. 'They're made to measure. And even if he did bump his head against a corner, there's no one to see it anyway.'

Reilly did not reply. But the thought that Jon was not lying as he should haunted him for a long time.

CHAPTER 11

The remains of the summer's floral splendour glowed against the red walls of Mrs Moreno's house. Above the doorbell was a porcelain sign in the shape of a salmon. INGERID AND JON LIVE HERE. Sejer and Skarre waited. It took some time before Ingerid opened the door and when she finally emerged, she did not speak a word. She disappeared inside.

'How are you?' Sejer asked.

She collapsed into an armchair, picked up a cushion and held it in front of her like a shield.

'How am I? I've lost Jon, and I've lost the rest of my life.'

Sejer protested. 'Don't think about the rest of your life,' he said. 'No one can look ahead when they're down.' He placed his hand on her arm.

'Jon kept a diary,' she said. 'Hanna Wigert brought it to the funeral yesterday. She found it in his room, in a drawer. It's on my bedside table.' Abruptly she got up from the armchair and went to her bedroom to fetch it.

Sejer touched the cover. The red fabric was coarse and quite plain.

'May I read it, please?' he asked.

'What good would that do?'

'We need it.'

She looked baffled.

'We'll talk more about it later,' he said. 'But first tell us about the funeral, please. Did you give Jon a lovely service?'

She pondered this for a while.

'I met Molly,' she said. 'She and Jon were very good friends. She brought along a terrier which caused something of a commotion. Have you heard about it?'

'Yes,' Sejer said. 'We've heard. How do you feel about what happened?'

'I thought it might be a sign. That all of us who knew Jon, we couldn't manage to hold on to him while he was alive. He got ill and he slipped through our fingers. And we didn't manage to keep hold of him in death either. We lost him to the earth, plain and simple. It says something about us.'

'What does it say?' Sejer asked.

'That we're all to blame.'

She fell silent. She waited for Sejer to move the conversation forward.

'When Jon was growing up, were you ever worried about him?' Sejer asked.

She smiled bleakly.

'Of course I was. He was my child. Is there anything we do but worry about them? There's so much they have to cope with,' she said. 'They have to find a space for themselves among their siblings, and in the classroom, and they have to survive in the playground. They have to find a peer group to belong to and a couple of close friends. They need an education and a job, and they need girl-friends. And children. Do you have children?' she asked.

'I have a daughter and a grandchild. They have managed all the things you mention. But I've never taken it for granted.'

He looked at her gravely.

'Ingerid. You need to listen to me. There is something I have to tell you and it's very confusing.'

She did not reply, but the cushion was now back in her lap.

'There are some details about Jon's death which we find unusual. We can't pinpoint anything in particular, yet we suspect that this case might be different, or that there's more to it than we first thought.'

'I don't follow,' she said.

'There are a few things about Jon's suicide which we don't understand.'

She let go of the cushion.

'What are you talking about? A few things? Are you saying someone else was involved? But there was no one up there, only Axel and Reilly. And they're his friends,' she said. 'They were very close. Are you out of your mind?'

Sejer placed his hand on the red diary.

'How much have you read?' he asked.

'Nothing,' she replied. 'Not a single line.'

'Are you scared?'

'Yes, I am.'

Memories from her own past surfaced and disturbed her. The summer she had travelled around Europe with a friend. One day they had found a wallet in a toilet. It had contained a thick bundle of notes, which after a brief discussion they chose to keep and later spent in an expensive restaurant. She remembered when she had had an abortion at nineteen. She was not even sure who the father was. Twice during her marriage to Tony Moreno she had been unfaithful. Both episodes had occurred when she had been travelling alone and she was drunk. When she recalled these incidents she felt woozy, and it struck her that she had not felt any remorse. Merely faint irritation, a slight jolt to the system. She had never, ever confided in anyone, simply stored it somewhere and later dismissed it as insignificant. But she remembered it now. She looked at the red diary. Did she have any sort of right to read Jon's confessions? She opened it up at the first page and read a few lines. Then she put it away, quickly, as though she had burned herself.

'I'll read it,' she said, 'and I'll let you know.'

CHAPTER 12

Molly Gram crossed the lawn in front of the hospital.

She walked diagonally towards the path, glancing briskly both to the left and right as she always did. Molly was seventeen years old, but her childish face, high forehead, slender body and the way she moved made her seem younger. She did not want to come across as womanly. She did not play on that side of herself because she had had her fingers burned. Instead she had assumed the role of small, grumpy girl. She took in everything as she walked. A limping man to her right, a couple strolling arm in arm across the car park. She assessed them as she moved. As far as she could see, there were no enemies around. Every time she left the ward she exposed herself to the outside world and its inhabitants, to the light and the wind. Something might come from above or something might attack her from the side. She felt safe only inside her room. Under her duvet. In the dark. With Melis.

She was outside now. She had finally reached the path. This was where she used to walk with Jon Moreno. Now the dog was her only companion. From time to time it would jump up and snap at her green skirt and she would tell it off in an affectionate voice. Little rascal, she said. Good doggy. She felt that Jon was somehow still with her, that his frail figure was at her side as usual, and she carried on an internal conversation with him.

Hi Jon, let's go for a walk. The weather is very nice. I like this time of year when it starts to get dark earlier. I couldn't find anyone who wanted to come for a walk with me. The others are so boring; they just hang out in the smoking room and can't be bothered to do anything. And they take no notice of what's going on outside. They don't know that monks are being killed in Burma and stuff like that.

Her inner voice grew quiet as if she lacked the strength to keep Jon alive. Her eyes soon began to dart around again, and she increased her speed. Melis had to run to keep up with her.

You and I would have been friends for life, she thought, I'm sure of that. But we didn't get enough time. Jon, I need you to listen to me now because there's something I have to tell you, something I've never told anyone. I want to kill myself too. But I'm afraid. I'm not that scared of dying, but I'm scared that I might change my mind. What if, say, I jump off a bridge and regret it and panic as I fall. Then I'll die with a terrible scream. I don't want to die screaming, it would be so embarrassing. People might think I'm some huge seagull as I flap past them, can you imagine that? And once I have made my decision, then I don't want to whine and moan about it, but to leave life behind with dignity. Or what if I take an overdose? And I have second thoughts and can't manage to make myself vomit. Imagine me kneeling in front of the toilet bowl, retching, how humiliating would that be? I can't see a future, only a road that is getting narrower and disappears round a bend and then into darkness, and I'm walking down that road alone. Damn you, Jon!

She sobbed as she walked on. She was quite deep into the forest now. Melis zigzagged; one moment he would appear on her right side, then ahead of her and then somewhat behind. A light breeze caused Molly's hair to flutter, and the leaves either side of the path rustled as if the forest were an animal stirring. Then she heard a different noise, the sound of a twig snapping. It can't be Melis, she thought, he's too light. She stopped abruptly and glanced over her shoulder. Was anyone there? What did they want? Melis, too, had stopped. His small ears had detected a sound. She increased her speed again. She was quite far from the hospital now. No one would hear her if she screamed. Were those footsteps? A muted shuffle and some dry cracks. Was it one of the men from the secure unit, she wondered, one of the lunatics? The patients in the secure unit had their own outside space, but sometimes they escaped. Molly could taste blood in her mouth. She turned around a second time, but there was nothing to see. Perhaps it was just a cat prowling through the scrub, nothing to get wound up about. Other people were out walking too; she did not own the forest or the path. Now calm down, Molly, she told herself.

Calm down, for God's sake!

But she could not calm down. And then she spotted a man some distance away. He stood motionless on the path. There was something familiar about him, and she searched her memory frantically.

Axel Frimann raised his hand and waved.

'Well, who would have thought it?' he said. 'It's Molly and Melis.'

He bowed solemnly. Molly could not work out what he was doing here, on her path. At her hospital. He took a few steps towards her. Molly stood very still as she watched him come closer.

'I didn't mean to frighten you,' he said, 'but I suddenly got it into my head to try this walk. You gave me the idea.'

Axel Frimann expected people to take the bait immediately, that they would be dangling from the hook on his first throw. But not Molly. Her kohl-rimmed eyes narrowed with scepticism.

'What did you make of the funeral?' Axel asked.

What does he mean? Molly wondered. Jon's funeral was terrible. She had never attended a sadder funeral in her entire life.

'I mean, the ceremony,' Axel said. 'The vicar's eulogy. It was lovely, wasn't it?'

'It was very ordinary,' Molly said.

'You think so?'

Axel fell silent. The sullen girl baffled him. He did not get the reaction he usually got when speaking to girls.

'You need to train that dog of yours,' he said. 'People are still talking about it, Jon hitting the ground.'

Molly shrugged. 'You should have kept steady,' she snapped.

'That mutt sank its teeth into Reilly's calf,' he said.

Molly looked down at her mutt.

'West Highland terrier,' she said. 'Eight kilos.'

Axel tried a different tack, a more friendly approach.

'It's hard to believe, isn't it? That he killed himself, I mean.'

Molly remembered Jon's voice. It always contained despair, suppressed tears.

'He was troubled by so many things,' she said.

Axel Frimann was on his guard now. 'That's what I've been thinking,' he said. 'That something must have happened, something he couldn't cope with. But I never found out what it was. He wouldn't even confide in his best friends. It's actually very hurtful to be kept at a distance. Did he confide in you?'

Molly stared down at her feet in the pink trainers. 'We spoke about most things,' she said.

Axel offered her his arm. 'Will you walk with me?' he asked.

Molly started walking in the opposite direction, back to the hospital. She walked quickly now. 'No, not at all.'

'Don't be so ill-tempered,' he said. 'There's no need. I was only asking.'

Molly strode on. Axel sauntered after her. Melis growled from the depths of his throat.

'Has Hanna Wigert been asking you a lot of questions?' Axel wanted to know. He was walking effortlessly beside her now.

Molly continued to walk as quickly as she could.

'About Jon, I mean,' Axel continued. 'If you have information which might explain his suicide.'

She stopped and gave him an irritated look. 'He was having a hard time. It's that simple. Jesus Christ, stop prying!'

'I'm sorry,' Axel said. 'I don't mean to interrogate you, but Jon was my best friend. It's a huge loss.'

'I'm quite insightful,' Molly said. 'All you've lost is control.'

That night she climbed into bed with Melis.

The darkness crept out from the corners and she felt the warmth from the panting dog. She was thinking of the things Jon had told her. I've got such a guilty conscience, he had said, I've made some big mistakes. I've discovered something terrible about myself. I'm a coward. This is what he used to say. But everybody makes mistakes and only a few of us are truly courageous, Molly thought, Jon must be thinking of something quite specific. She was startled when the door opened. A beam of light fell across the floor and she saw Ruth, the night nurse. Melis raised his head to suss out the intruder. Ruth entered and looked down at Molly in the bed. Molly had removed the black make-up and without it she was another person, a pale and blurry child against the white bed linen. Ruth perched on the edge of the bed and Molly clasped her arm with both hands.

'You're so good to touch,' she said. 'You're like warm dough.'

Ruth laughed heartily. She carried some extra weight, and she was used to Molly being direct.

'So what's keeping you awake?' she asked.

'I'm thinking about Jon. And everything Jon said. And how to manage without him.'

'There are other people out there you can trust,' Ruth said. 'Time is on your side. You'll find someone.'

'But no one is like Jon,' Molly said. 'And what we had, I'll never find that again.'

Ruth patted Molly's cheek with her chubby hand.

'Did he ever tell you what was on his mind?' she asked.

Molly sat up in bed. She pulled the duvet to her chin. 'Yesterday I saw a man on TV,' she said. 'He was one of those explorers. He was going to live in the wilderness for thirty days. In Canada. Where the Inuit live. He packed everything he would need on a sledge. It weighed a hundred kilos. He could barely drag it across the ice.'

Ruth waited for her to continue.

'Jon's conscience was that bad,' Molly said. 'He had so much to drag along.'

Ruth sighed. 'He never should have gone to that cabin,' she said. 'He didn't want to. Perhaps he sensed that something might happen.

All the staff here at Ladegården feel responsible. We so wanted him to go. God knows what we were thinking. But if he had killed himself here on the ward, we would have felt even more responsible. And if we had discharged him and he had killed himself afterwards, then we would also have felt responsible. And if he had done it at home in his own bed, then his mother would have felt responsible. Do you see what I'm saying? That's how it is with suicides.'

Molly held Melis up to her face. She inhaled his smell. It made her think of sweet spices.

'If you like, we can visit his grave one day,' Ruth said. 'You and I together. We can take some flowers. We can say a few words and imagine that they'll reach Jon. You never can tell.'

Molly shook her head. 'He won't hear one word,' she said. 'Of that I'm certain.'

'Molly,' Ruth implored. 'You need to hold on to some mystery in your life. You don't know everything.'

'Those friends of his,' Molly said. 'Do you think they were good friends?'

Ruth frowned. 'You mean the ones who took him to the cabin? I imagine so. They had known each other a long time. Why do you ask?'

Molly returned Melis to the foot of her bed. 'Not all friends are good ones,' she said. 'Some are there purely out of habit. Or because they benefit from knowing you.'

Ruth listened in silence.

'They profit from you,' Molly continued. 'Or they need you for some reason. To outsiders, it looks like a friendship.'

Ruth tried to follow her thoughts.

'But if Jon didn't want to be a part of that trio,' she said, 'then why didn't he end the friendship?'

'Perhaps that was what he was trying to do,' Molly said. 'Perhaps he sought refuge here, at the hospital.'

'You're saying he was escaping from his friends?'

'He was trying to hide here,' Molly said, 'but they came and got him.'

73

'Why do you say that?'

Molly tossed her head. 'I notice things.'

'You're going to be all right, Molly,' Ruth said, 'because you're sharp.'

'I'm not going to be all right,' Molly said, fluffing her pillow gently. 'I'm going to be here at Ladegården for ever. In this bed. In this room. With you.'

Ruth was wise and so she did not protest. 'Perhaps,' she said. 'Perhaps we'll both be here for ever, you and I.'

She got up from Molly's bed. Her heavy body moved across the floor.

'You remind me of a container ship at sea,' Molly said.

Ruth grunted by way of reply.

'You lie quite low in the water. And you're heeling a bit. But your sails are full, I'll give you that.'

'Go to sleep,' Ruth laughed, 'and give that sharp tongue of yours a rest.'

CHAPTER 13

Ingerid Moreno was standing by the window.

Her hands were resting on the windowsill. She still wore Tony Moreno's ring on her right hand. He had left her, but she liked the ring with the pink pearl. Her eyes swept across the garden and the other houses in the residential area where she lived. Everything was pretty, well maintained and green, every hedge trimmed, every fruit tree pruned, because the people who lived there were hard-working. For a long time she admired birds on a branch, the early autumn foliage and the damp grass. Tumbling clouds, the sound of music from an open window, all these things Jon had lost. She turned and glanced at the coffee table where the diary glowed red. I may not have the right, she thought, but I'm a human being in need. She curled up in an armchair with the diary on her lap. On the back of it she discovered a white label with the text MADE IN CHINA and also a yellow price sticker. This is Jon's life, she mused, and the price is 29.99 kroner. She switched on the reading lamp and opened the first page.

My name is Jon Moreno. I'm a patient at Ladegården Psychiatric Hospital and I have sat down to write. Is there any point in writing things down?

Will everything become clearer, will it be a relief? Does it serve as a confession, and as a result will I be forgiven for everything? I need absolution. But I have ended up in a situation where it is unobtainable. People will say that my actions were unforgivable and that is true. But if I don't confess then I will go tainted to my grave. I don't believe in God, but I cannot bear the thought of being consumed by remorse in my final hour. But then there are always other considerations. There are other people and their dreams and plans for the future. Should I destroy even more than I have already? I'm not very strong. Sometimes, at night, when I lie in the darkness, tossing and turning, I end up praying to God anyway. It helps for a few minutes. Then I feel even more of a fraud than before because I'm praying to someone I don't believe in, but then again He might exist and He is watching my hypocrisy and that makes it even worse. When I finally fall asleep I have nightmares. Someone is hammering on my door, they have come for me and it's all over. Perhaps I have this dream because deep down this is what I want. Someone to expose me finally and call me to account. That black December night haunts every second of my life. When I woke up the next day, I felt confused. I tried to recall what had happened. Did we drive off the road and end up in a ditch? Perhaps that's one way of looking at it: we lost our way and I'm still in that ditch. I have been so privileged. I had a good childhood. My mum taught me right from wrong. All my life I have imagined that my morals were high, that I was decent and honest and truthful. But what happened to my morals when I was tested? A nasty voice started whispering in my ear: it was all right to run away, besides there were more of us, a lot was at stake. I don't understand where that voice came from, I didn't know it even existed. Perhaps it had been dormant for a long time and then, when I needed it, it started its vile whispering. Reilly does have a conscience, he is a humble guy, but Axel Frimann is a Master of the Universe. It was a battle of wills I was bound to lose. No matter how I handle this I will be exposed to contempt. At times I can see the contours of a devil, someone who watched us that night and laid a trap for us. I know that's nonsense. Life is full of coincidences. Yet I feel so bitter because we're not bad people. How can you know you're a good person if your life has been nothing but plain sailing?

CHAPTER 14

Axel Frimann had his own office in the advertising agency Repeat, and he had personally designed its elegant interior. That was how he saw himself: he had style and class – and most people agreed with him. This was Axel Frimann's kingdom. In here he ruled supreme, in here he was creative and inspired, in here he would seduce people through the power of advertising, and he was an expert. He understood its psychology and mechanisms. He knew the power of humour and the importance of laughter, which made people open up, allowing the message to pour in, slip past every barrier. He was doodling on a notepad when one of his colleagues entered.

'It looks like we're getting the new razor account,' he said. 'It's made in Norway. It's called Hellrazor. Cool name, don't you think?'

He waved a sheet of paper. 'They hope to force Gillette out of the Norwegian market, no less, and that's why they've hired us. So you know what your remit is. And they don't want us replicating an old pompous approach. We've got to come up with something completely new.'

'Hellrazor?' Axel enthused. 'The razor from hell. Those guys have a sense of humour, we can work with that.'

He snatched the sheet. He studied the picture and the text, the razor, its features and hyped-up superiority.

'Let me guess,' he said. 'Hellrazor shaves closer than any other razor?'

His colleague shrugged. 'I presume so. After all, it's brand new.'

Axel shook his head and smiled. 'But, really, how much closer can they shave?'

His colleague gave him a baffled look. 'I suppose they're using new and better materials,' he said. 'Who cares? All we've got to do is make sure it sells, and better than Gillette, if possible.'

'Then this is my idea,' Axel said, 'to get the message across once and for all.'

He reclined in his chair and took a deep breath.

'A couple is asleep in bed. Black silk bed linen, white walls and curtains. Sun beaming through the window. Are you listening?'

'Yes,' his colleague said.

'The alarm clock goes off, the man wakes up and embraces his beloved. He is unshaven, so we add a horrible rasping sound effect – sandpaper on sandpaper for example. The woman pushes him away and goes into the bathroom. He follows her. The bathroom', he added, 'has black tiles and recessed lighting. White china suite from Porsgrund and a lily in a wall-mounted vase. The man puts on a dressing gown and stands in front of the mirror. He picks up the razor while she cleans her teeth.'

Axel Frimann paused.

'And then?' his colleague said. 'What happens?'

'He's finished shaving. He goes to her for another hug. After all, he's just shaved. But above the collar of his dressing gown all we see is his skull.'

'Eh?'

'The razor has gone right to the bone,' Axel said. 'All we see is his smooth, white skull. And then a voiceover at the end: "Hellrazor. You'll never have a closer shave."'

'Pull the other one,' his colleague responded. 'It's got bells on.'

'I'm deadly serious,' Axel Frimann said. 'That kind of ad would match the name, and we're talking about a bloody close shave, aren't we? So we'll give them a skeleton. We've got to address a younger, trendier market, and humour is very important.'

His colleague disappeared, slamming the door behind him. Ten seconds later he opened it again and looked in.

'That's not an ad,' he said. 'It's a mockery.'

He disappeared for the second time. Axel, however, was

delighted with the idea. An ad like this would get everyone talking because it was outrageous, daring and witty. It would win awards. He chewed his pen. The violent burst of creativity had left him, he was alone and it grew silent around him. The silence made him feel like he was floating. He was overcome by the urge to bark orders, slam his fist on the table, bang on a door to show he was still here and still in charge. Something had started to trouble his otherwise tightly controlled universe: a tiny prickle when someone knocked on the door, a pounding heart whenever the telephone rang. A feeling that someone was following him when he walked down the street, a new awareness of sounds and footsteps, at night thoughts of detectives in an office discussing whether Jon really killed himself. Axel Frimann was restless. The light from the window irritated him, and then the silence was broken by a series of noises from the big building, doors slamming, telephones ringing, someone laughing – what the hell were they laughing at?

His world was cracking up, flaking like dry paint. He experienced a heightened sensitivity everywhere as if life, which had so far never touched him, was suddenly sticking needles into his body. He raised his hands and studied them closely: the pale skin on his palms, the fine lines. Many of the lines were broken, weren't they? He leaned forward and rested his head on the desk, pressing his cheek against the warm wood. He picked up the scent of oak and furniture oil. I'm sitting here, Axel Frimann thought, and I'm alive. How does the body know when the end has come? Who decides when the heart beats for the last time, is there a code deep inside us, a limited amount of energy which we can consume, as when you wind up a toy?

Axel Frimann was not used to contemplating death. It made him edgy. His heartbeat felt a little irregular, he thought, his forehead clammy. He was also aware of a slight toothache, a molar in his lower jaw, only mild pain, though, of no consequence. He straightened up in his chair. Baffled, he stroked his chin. Yes, intermittent pain as though a tiny creature lived inside his tooth. He imagined a tadpole wiggling, not constantly, but at regular intervals. It became a more niggling pain, or rather it was like a faint vibration at the root of the tooth. He bent over his papers to continue his work, trying to focus on Hellrazor. He was still adamant that his skeleton in a dressing gown concept would work. But soon the niggling turned into more persistent pain. Axel Frimann felt a surge of irritation. He did not allow unexpected things to happen. Either I'll have to go home, he thought, or I need to take some painkillers. This is bloody annoying.

He left his office and went outside, where his secretary, Ella, was sitting in front of her computer.

'Do you have some paracetamol? Axel asked.

She gave Axel a warm smile and picked up her handbag. She rummaged in it for a moment. He could hear clattering from its depths.

'Sorry, I'm afraid not. Try Margaret.'

Axel plodded down the corridor. His normally broad shoulders drooped. He knocked on Margaret's door before entering. She was standing by the photocopier. Steam was coming from a mug of coffee on her desk.

'What's the matter?' she asked.

'I've got toothache,' Axel explained. 'Do you have some paracetamol? Or something stronger?'

'Hang on, I'll check,' she said and sashayed over to her desk. She had no chance with Axel, but she had never stopped hoping, and her bottom was undeniably her best asset. She pulled out a drawer and searched among pens and paper. She dumped a pile of stationery on the table, a pair of scissors, a glue stick, sticky tape and a box of paperclips.

'I usually have some,' she said, 'but I've run out. Ask Jørgen. Jørgen suffers from migraines. He's bound to have an emergency supply.'

Axel Frimann knocked on Jørgen's door.

'Jesus Christ, what's wrong with you?'

Axel slumped in a chair. He pressed his hand to his cheek and gave him a suffering look.

'Something's wrong with my jaw,' he said. 'I've got this stabbing pain. I think it's an infected root, I can feel it all the way down my jaw. Do you have some paracetamol?'

But he left Jørgen's office empty-handed too. Axel had to go back. He shuffled down the corridors, opening one door after another pleading his case like a beggar. There was the guy in the basement office, he remembered, who delivered the post. Didn't he have rheumatism? And then there was Randi in the canteen, she was over sixty and must be afflicted by a range of ailments, wear and tear, he thought, pain in her neck and shoulders. The reception desk on the ground floor was staffed by a thin girl who always looked very pale. Her face was a mesh of green veins and her hands always trembled. Anaemic, he thought, and anorexic. Stress and possibly headaches. He wandered down the corridors, knocking on door after door, but everyone shook their head regretfully.

No one could put Axel out of his misery.

CHAPTER 15

Dear diary,

I've started looking at people as if seeing them for the first time. When I go out for a walk in the hospital park, I notice that they are lit differently. It's something to do with the way the sun hits them, it makes their faces glow. That guy on the bicycle, for example, who passed me this morning, he would never have acted as carelessly as I did. He would have taken responsibility and done the right thing. I could see it in his eyes and in the way he held his head. Because he knows he is worth something, he knows that he is a good person. In his life there are clear rules which he always follows. The old lady holding the granny trolley who came out of the shop, she is bound to be the sort who helps insects to their freedom. And the shop assistant in the baker's where I bought rolls yesterday, the girl with the round cheeks, she is goodness itself. I used to be one of them. Once I belonged to this exclusive group of people with a clear conscience. It's hard to look people in the eye. My voice has lost its power. I'm waiting for the axe to fall, and I know it will. How quickly it can change, the life we think has been marked out for us. We start the journey with good intentions, the gift our parents bequeathed us. And then, someone snaps their fingers and we find ourselves sidetracked; we end up in a foreign country. Suddenly we think differently about everything, we are in alien territory and other rules apply there. I no longer recognise my own life. I have lost my way, and the thing that happened is not fading away, either. I'm almost too scared to open a newspaper or switch on the radio because of what they might say and how much they will have found out. It's a miracle that I still walk around a free man.

CHAPTER 16

The dentist diagnosed that Axel had an infected wisdom tooth. The tooth was on the left side of his mouth.

'From the outside everything looks fine,' the dentist said, 'but it's rotten to the core. It's often the way,' he joked.

He held up the X-ray up to the light and pointed.

'I've never seen the like, though,' he said. 'It's aggressive. I'll need to open it up and clean it out. And I'm afraid you'll have to brace yourself for a certain amount of discomfort.'

Axel's cheeks were flushed. He was furious because he had been forced to submit to another man, another man's breath and another man's hands. He was anaesthetised and the whole of his lower jaw felt numb, and he could not feel his tongue. I'll be drooling like an idiot all day, he thought. After the treatment he was given some painkillers, but they only dulled the ache slightly. He drove home, opened a bottle of Gran Feudo, collapsed on his sofa and poured himself a glass of wine, which he gulped down. The roots of his teeth were throbbing, sending waves of pain to his head; violent, burning spasms which took his breath away. He had heard that such infections could spread and attack the whole jaw, and for a moment he panicked. He imagined that his chin would crumble, that it could never be repaired, and that he, Axel Frimann of the fine profile, would end up a chinless freak. He massaged his jaw and felt very sorry for himself. The pain, which originated in the roots of his teeth, found its way to the top of his head, where it threatened his pride. Axel Frimann was a wronged man. Something he could not control had disregarded his excellence and decided to act as it pleased. And this something cared nothing for his exalted position but tormented him as though he was just anyone.

The doorbell rang. He knew it would be Reilly.

'What are you on this time?' Axel asked when he saw his swimmy eyes.

'Georgia Home Boy,' Reilly said.

'And what is that?'

'GHB. Or Salty Water,' Reilly said. 'Or Jib. Known and loved by all. What's up?'

He stepped inside.

Axel wanted to say that he had toothache. However, he started telling Reilly a different story, and he did not understand why. He was not in the habit of confiding in anyone. People who opened up were like babies spewing milk. But it was as if the pain unlocked something he would normally have kept quiet about. There was an ache inside him which he had ignored for a long time.

'I went to the hospital yesterday,' he said. 'To see my dad.'

Reilly gave him a look of surprise. Axel never spoke about his father. Perhaps he was ashamed of him or perhaps his illness was too hard for him to deal with. In just a few seconds he had been robbed of his father, a handsome man, who had suddenly collapsed in a ditch. He had lain in a hospital bed ever since, pale and shapeless like sausage meat.

'I'll tell you what happened,' Axel said, 'so that you know. We were walking down the road, my dad and I. Four years ago. It was summer. I had come to visit them at their holiday cottage. We had gone to buy some eggs from a nearby farm. My mum needed them for baking. Idyllic, don't you think? Father and son on a country road on a warm, sunny day. He was fifty-three years old. Fifty-three, Reilly. He was a good-looking man, he was still in great shape and everything. You remember that, don't you, that he was a good-looking man?'

Reilly nodded. He had splayed his feet to keep his balance. His head was spinning and he would have preferred to sit down, but he didn't dare move.

'It was a warm afternoon,' Axel said. 'I remember a few details.

Insects. Stinging nettles by the roadside. An awful lot of stinging nettles. They have their own special smell, by the way, did you know that? You can make soup from them, but I can't imagine it tastes very good.'

Reilly was unsure where this was going. Not that the business with Axel's father was a secret; everyone knew he was a goner, that he would never walk again. But Axel was so pale and his eyes so black, as though he might attack the first person he saw. And I would be the first person, Reilly thought. He retreated a step, just to be on the safe side.

'We were walking down the road,' Axel said. 'We were in the middle of a conversation. My dad was quite talkative; he always had something to say, an opinion about something or other. A point of view. Suddenly he shot off to the left and then he simply ran into the ditch head first. I've never seen anything so terrifying. It was like the air going out of an inflatable toy. All I could think about was the stinging nettles. He was wearing a short-sleeved shirt. When I bent over, I noticed his jaw had slackened, it was disgusting. On one side. Do you know what I mean?'

Reilly knew. He saw Axel touch his jaw. He moved to the wall for support. The drugs he had taken were making him dizzy.

'His face was completely distorted,' Axel said. 'I didn't know what was happening, so I phoned for help. It was a long wait. I couldn't get anything out of him. I just squatted down in the sun thinking that someone had beaten him up. Because that's what it looked like. Someone had given him a beating that he would never recover from. I didn't know exactly what had happened, but I was certain of this: he had been destroyed. He was gurgling and waving one hand as though he wanted me to go away. I didn't know what to do and I couldn't bear to look at him. I had to get up and walk a little way down the road, but I kept hearing the noises he was making. Then they came to get him. They rolled him on to a stretcher and later into a bed. That was the last time we had a conversation.'

'But he does make sounds?' Reilly tried. Gravity making its way through his drug-induced haze.

'Yes, but they're completely meaningless,' Axel interrupted him. 'Just gurgling and grunting. It would be better if he would just shut up. I can hardly bear to look at him, either. I don't even know if he is pleased to see me. I don't think so. I don't think he gives a toss. Everything about it is embarrassing. It's humiliating and revolting. He needs help with everything. From strangers.'

'Does he know who you are?' Reilly asked cautiously.

'Yes.'

'How do you know?'

'He starts to cry.'

Axel paused. The pain hammered away at his jaw and he was about to be overcome by a violent attack of self-pity.

'He's been lying in that bed for four years,' he said.

'Mm,' Reilly sighed.

'He's got bedsores,' Axel said. 'Lots of them. They're really deep.'

Reilly nodded for the second time. He had never seen bedsores because his job was moving beds around, but he understood that if you spent years lying in a warm bed, then your skin would not get the circulation that it needed, especially not where the skin was stretched tightly across the bones. It grew red and tender and eventually tiny cracks would form. That was how he imagined it.

'They're deep,' Axel repeated. 'His body is riddled with holes and the holes have turned into long tunnels.'

Reilly's eyes widened. He visualised the long tunnels through the haze, and he began to feel queasy.

'It's like an eel has bored through him,' Axel said, 'and it's no use closing the sores, they're too big. I was there once when they changed his bandages. They stank of decay. He's completely perforated. Like a worm-eaten apple.'

'What's this really about?' Reilly asked. 'You're completely manic.'

'Infected wisdom tooth.'

'Christ Almighty. Does it hurt?'

'Like hell,' Axel replied.

'You might have told me straight away,' Reilly said. 'Instead you go on about your perforated dad.'

Axel groaned. 'I just wanted to make a point,' he said. 'My dad did everything right. His whole life. Because he believed it would lead to something good. But I've learned my lesson. I don't owe anyone anything. I reserve the right to make my own rules. I've never signed any contracts and I've never made any promises. I could do the right thing my whole life, but no one would reward me for it.'

'I'm not sure where you're going with this,' Reilly stuttered.

'I'm not going anywhere,' Axel barked. 'I can give everything I own to a poor man in Africa, and the next second I might get run over by a truck. That's how it is and we have to accept it. So don't ask me to make moral decisions! And don't you whine on about Jon!'

Reilly opened his mouth to say something, but Axel continued, his eyes shining.

'Don't you dare quote the Koran!' he yelled.

Reilly pulled a chair over to the window. Axel had a view of the river. They saw a tanker move slowly, its lights shining. A long silence followed Axel's bitter rant.

'What do you think it's carrying?' Reilly asked and pointed.

Axel massaged his jaw and said nothing.

'Chemicals, probably,' Reilly mused.

'I don't give a damn about its cargo,' Axel said. 'For all I care it could be chocolate mice.'

'The crews of chemical tankers become sterile,' Reilly said. 'They never have kids. By the way, we don't import chocolate mice,' he added, 'we make our own. It's Nidar isn't it, who makes the mice?'

Axel focused on his breathing. He knew that oxygen was important when it came to pain management. 'I need to talk to Hanna Wigert,' he said. 'I need to know if she suspects anything. I need to be in control.'

'We lost that in December,' Reilly said.

Axel swallowed a large mouthful of red wine.

'It's worth keeping your eyes open,' he said. 'And then there's Molly. I don't trust her either. Girls like her have a vivid imagination. And fantasies can turn into rumours.'

Reilly shook his head in disbelief. 'You had best take an axe and kill off all of Ladegården just to be on the safe side. Cut them down. Right at the root. Best kill Ingerid, too, she's probably reading Jon's diary this very minute.'

Again he looked out at the huge ship. The child in him marvelled that it was possible for thousands of tonnes to float. Axel would explain in his usual way that it was a matter of even weight distribution, it was always about that. Also, when you move through enemy territory, he would say, it's a question of putting your feet down with care.

'I fancy working on a boat,' Reilly said. 'Being in constant motion, under the sky, seeing new cities, new landscapes. Standing on the top deck at night and gazing at the stars. The feeling of floating, drifting, not being tied to anything. They earn good money too. Not that I care about that.'

Here he glanced at Axel. '"Better starve free than be a fat slave,"' he said.

'I'm starting to get fed up with the Koran,' Axel said.

'It's not from the Koran. It's just an old proverb.'

They were silent. Reilly savoured the gentle haze that filled his head and made him feel brave and brimming with confidence. The drugs dulled his conscience, and he became generous and indulgent towards himself. I haven't really done anything wrong, he thought, I'm a victim. Of circumstance. Of course I bloody am. He looked out at the river again. Then he burst out laughing at the idea that the huge ship might be loaded with chocolate mice after all. He imagined the mice escaping through the packaging and darting around the hold, crawling around the boat and spilling out on to the deck while the crew pressed themselves against the rail and watched the invasion.

'Could you shut up, please,' Axel said. 'I'm in pain.'

Reilly calmed down and felt remorseful.

'I'm really sorry about your dad,' he said.

Axel blanked him. Reilly kept looking at the tanker. Her slow progress, her beauty and elegance on the grey water mesmerised him.

'I've never laid a hand on anyone in my life,' Axel said out of the blue. 'Not on Jon, or anyone else.'

Reilly wanted to reply, but the drugs had made him sluggish and he was incapable of formulating a sentence.

'Have I ever laid a hand on anyone?' Axel asked.

'Not really sure,' Reilly mumbled.

'Not really sure?' Axel said. 'What sort of an answer is that?'

But Reilly kept his mouth shut. When Axel lost his temper, it was best to lie low for a while.

A wide, frothing stream flowed into Glitter Lake, and on the bank a woman was watching the sky. She was one of those people whom life had treated well, so she had a little smile at the corner of her mouth. It came naturally to her. Behind her lay a hill surrounded by dense vegetation and further away a small sandy beach. She was sitting on a rock. Next to her was a canvas bag in which she kept a watercolour block, paints and brushes. She got water from the lake. Glitter Lake was a pretty landscape. She had an eye for detail and she was absorbed by the light, which changed constantly as the clouds were driven across the sky by a mild breeze. From time to time the sun would break through, and she would close her eyes, relishing its warmth. There was a green and black whirlpool where the stream poured into the lake, and the churning water had created a wide tuft of foam. A gnarled root from a tree stuck out of the whirlpool. This foreground constituted the subject. The root which had anchored itself in the mud was almost a sculpture in itself. She decided to tone down the cloud formations lest they distort the balance of the composition. The focal point should be low, the sky should play second fiddle. She placed the pad in her lap and started outlining the scene with a soft pencil, and anyone looking over her shoulder would have seen that she was a skilled artist. She did not hesitate for a second. There was a direct link between her eyes and her hand. While she worked, she enjoyed all the elements as different voices in an orchestra: the wind, the roaring water and the scent of grass. The whirlpool, she thought, it looks like a well, and the big tuft of foam looks like the cream on an Irish coffee. The root resembles an arm with an accusing finger. She imagined it was pointing to something far out in the lake. Look, it was saying, look out there! She stared with one hand shielding her eyes, but she saw nothing, only the glittering surface from which the lake took its name. She continued to draw. The smile at the corner of her mouth remained, she was so pleased with it all, with the lake and her own talent.

When she had finished sketching the scene, she went down to fill a plastic cup with water, and then she mixed colours in the lid of her watercolour box. Sounds from the forest reached her: a dove, a woodpecker at a tree trunk. All the time her brush raced across the paper in quick, light strokes, the thin marten hairs created circles and waves, saturated with green and blue. She had been painting Glitter Lake for years. At home she had countless variations painted under different conditions and seasons. When the picture was finished, she rested it against a stone. She took a few steps back and assessed her own work with a clear, cool head. I'm a decent artist, she thought, and smiled at her own cheek. She saw that it was not perfect, the root sticking out of the whirlpool really did look like an arm, as though a body had floated by and got caught. She turned abruptly and stared across the water. No, it can't be, she thought. Nevertheless she went down to the water to investigate, gingerly stepping out on to some rocks and squatting down. In the slippery green and black she saw a tooth.

It was the body of a man, and he seemed to be of foreign origin. His long stay in the water had made his skin permeable and his body had bloated to almost twice its natural size. This made him look big and sturdy. In reality he was short and slender. He was wearing jeans and a thin windbreaker, and all they found in his pocket was a key attached to a bit of string. The key was made by TrioVing.

The report from the Institute of Forensic Medicine began as follows: male, possibly Asian, one hundred and sixty-seven centimetres tall. Teeth intact and in good condition with no fillings. No surgical scars, no tattoos, no moles, no broken bones. Age: under twenty. They had compared their findings to the missing persons register. And they were creating a DNA profile.

Sejer and Skarre were about to leave the office. They got their coats and Skarre fished out a jelly baby from a bag.

'I used to like the green ones best,' he said, 'but now I prefer the orange ones.'

Sejer watched him as he munched the small gelatinous figure. 'I imagine they all taste the same,' he declared, 'but, of course, you expect something different from a red jelly baby and a yellow one.'

This statement made Skarre peer into the bag with a worried expression. 'I need to work something out,' he said.

'Why?'

'Because we've found a man in a lake. Do you follow?'

'I'm not a mind reader,' Sejer remarked.

'It reminds me I'm going to die one day,' Skarre said. 'I'm going to die, but it doesn't worry me unduly.'

Sejer shuffled through his papers and his eyes fell on the report from the Institute of Forensic Medicine.

'But then I think beyond that,' Skarre continued. 'Some years later those who knew me will die too, and then there won't be anyone left to remember me. Or who'll visit my grave. Jacob Skarre? people will say. Never heard of him.'

'That's very sad,' Sejer agreed.

'And then we reach the worst part,' Skarre said. 'My grave will be reused. And I won't exist anywhere – not in other people's memories and not in the cemetery.'

'Why are you tormenting yourself with such notions?' Sejer asked. 'After all, you're a Christian. You're going to find eternal life.'

'I doubt that,' Skarre confessed.

'But the Bible says so,' Sejer objected. 'Do you simply pick bits and pieces and stick them together just as you please?'

'Yes,' Skarre admitted. 'That's how we do it.' He let himself fall into a chair.

'All of mankind will disappear too,' Sejer said. 'One day only insects will be left. And no one will know that we were ever here.'

'But we were a great idea,' Skarre said.

The telephone rang and he answered it. 'Forensics,' he said. 'Snorrason.'

Sejer took the receiver and grabbed a pen.

'I've got a preliminary autopsy report for you,' Snorrason said. 'I've examined his lungs. And it's hard to draw any definite conclusions after such a long time, but there is evidence to suggest he was dead when he fell in the water.'

'Then we have a case.'

'Probably.'

'Any idea who he is?'

'Not so far. I'll let you know.'

'Cuts? Bruises?'

'Doesn't look like it. I can find no internal or external injuries.'

'Strangulation?'

'Unlikely.'

'Toxins?'

'We've sent samples off for testing. They'll take time.'

'So you can't tell me anything about the cause of death?'

'Not yet. And I'm sorry to have to mention this, but it's possible that we might fail. It does happen. This young Asian man is an enigma.'

'Let's hope you come up with something,' Sejer said. 'Somewhere his parents are waiting for him.'

'Everyone who comes to me had parents,' Snorrason said.

Sejer and Skarre left the office and went out into the corridor. For years they had walked like this, side by side, sometimes in animated discussion, sometimes silent as now. When Sejer suddenly stumbled, Skarre automatically rushed to support him. Sejer slumped against the wall. He stood with his eyes closed for a few seconds.

'What is it?' Skarre said.

Sejer touched his head. His vision was blurred. 'Oh, nothing. I don't know.' Baffled, he rubbed his eyes. The dizziness began to subside and Skarre, who was standing in front of him, came into focus once more.

'Are you ill?'

'Certainly not.'

Sejer wanted to walk on. He did so cautiously. Skarre hurried after him.

'Haven't you eaten?' he asked. He had never seen the inspector lose his balance like that.

'Of course I've eaten,' Sejer said. 'Now don't fuss.'

They had reached the lift. Sejer had regained his composure. He pushed the button and below the lift whirred into motion.

'I imagine your blood pressure plummeted,' Skarre muttered.

'Get in the lift,' Sejer said.

They entered the lift. Sejer studied his younger colleague and decided to confide in him.

'My stumbling is unlikely to be serious,' he said. 'But every morning when I go to the bathroom, something unpleasant happens. When I look in the mirror, I see this older man staring back at me. He seems familiar. He has penetrating eyes as though he knows me better than I do. There's something about that man that rattles me,' Sejer said. 'Something that makes me want to show him the door.'

Skarre looked at the grey-haired inspector.

'I've known that man a long time,' he said. 'He's quite all right, really.'

CHAPTER 17

Dear diary,

Every one of us harbours guilt, every one of us has sinned in some way or other. I'm not talking about original sin, I don't believe in that, but we're not very old before we sin for the first time. We're not very old before we lie or steal. Or speak ill of someone. We have all hated someone and felt envy surge through our bodies. We have all been greedy, we have all taken something that was not rightfully ours. We have all wanted to lash out or scream, we have all felt that rage inside us and perhaps thought the sensation felt good. Yet some people dance their way through life. And those who ought to feel shame, haven't got the sense to feel it. Nevertheless I can forgive myself for most things, not for what happened in December, but for everything else. That I nicked money from Mum's purse to buy chocolate when I was a boy, as kids do. Perhaps I ought to have told her, though I imagine she already knows because mums are canny; they're always ahead of you. It would have been good to have something to blame it on, a bad childhood, or bad friends. Dad left us, but Mum never gave me cause to miss him. She was a mother and father to me. So if I end up in court I will hang my head and no defence counsel will find mitigating circumstances. I wonder what it's like to lose someone, never having a grave, a concrete place to go – a small plot to weed, a place to plant something which can grow where the deceased rests. Not to have any of these things, but to live in ignorance while your imagination runs riot. When I think about that I feel ill, and I am consumed with such self-loathing that I can barely breathe. My disgust with myself thickens my blood. When I wake up in the morning the sheet is soaked with contempt.

Reilly just gets high. I can understand why, I would like to have something like that, something that quells the despair. When it comes to Axel, I find it hard to fathom him, but he takes after his mother, and she's a bitch, someone who just takes what they want without a thought for anyone else. So it runs in the family. Devil eggs breed devil children, Reilly says. He's always got something apt to say because he reads so much. Reilly is a slow and meek guy. Sometimes he seems indifferent or lethargic, but perhaps he will surprise us after all. Axel is the boss and always has been, but Reilly works away quietly on the side. I would not rule out the possibility that he might do something one day. Something dramatic which will upset the equilibrium.

CHAPTER 18

The pain in Axel's wisdom tooth grew steadily worse and on the third day when he came home from work, he pulled off his clothes and went straight to bed. He switched off the light. He curled up against the wall. He lay with a flannel pressed against his cheek and at regular intervals he went to the bathroom to rinse it in cold water and wring it out. This relieved the pain for a few minutes. He moved the cloth around his face, across his cheeks and forehead, while he emitted faint groans. The pain filled his head. It made him tense his muscles, and the tension increased the pain. It was a vicious circle. When the doorbell rang, he stayed in bed. But whoever it was refused to go away and eventually he staggered out into the hall.

'Bloody hell, you look a sight,' Reilly said.

'It's spreading,' Axel groaned. 'It's spreading across my jaw.'

'Shouldn't you go to the hospital, then?'

'I don't know. I feel nauseous. I'm clammy with sweat.'

Axel leaned against the wall for support. He stared at a point on the floor which started to move as he watched. It was a spider. He squashed it with his heel.

'They've found a body,' Reilly said. 'In Glitter Lake.'

Axel's jaw dropped. 'You're kidding.'

'They've found a body. They say he's Asian.'

Axel froze. For the first time in a long while the unbearable pain faded into the background.

'Come on,' he said. 'Let's sit down.'

He collapsed in a chair, still pressing the cloth against his cheek. Axel's furniture was covered in buffalo hide. He enjoyed the idea that the armchairs and sofa had once thundered across the savannah. Now it felt that way, literally, as if the chair was moving beneath him. The flannel against his cheek had long since reached room temperature, but it helped nevertheless. It was a symbol, like a bandage on a wound. The squashed spider was still stuck to his heel.

'It can't be him,' he mumbled.

'Of course it can,' Reilly said.

'And when will they know who he is?'

'It'll probably take some time,' Reilly suggested. 'I imagine he's badly decomposed now as well; he's been lying there for months.'

He pulled off his long coat.

'They have to be certain. But once they know his identity, they'll start working their way back to 19 December. They won't give up. They'll find us, Axel.'

He went to the window and looked out. No huge tankers on the river today, only smaller boats.

'I wonder what kind of view I'll have from my cell,' he muttered.

'Please would you shut up?' Axel groaned. 'My throat hurts too. I think the infection has spread to my throat. I wonder if I'll get blood poisoning.'

He moved the cloth to his forehead and wiped away some beads of sweat.

'So they've found a bloody Chink?'

Reilly turned. 'I don't know where he's from,' he said, 'but it doesn't look good for us.'

'Guilt has to be proven beyond all reasonable doubt,' Axel said. 'We have many advantages. They'll have to work very hard.'

'What about the truth?' Reilly said gravely.

Axel waved irritably with his other arm. 'You're so naive,' he said. 'Where do you think the truth will get us? Do you think truth is a limousine that will take us to a five-star hotel with a lobby full of cheering fans? The truth is unpleasant, Reilly. Ingerid Moreno doesn't want it. We owe it to Jon to preserve his good name. Remember, that name will live on for generations.'

'You're thinking very long term,' Reilly remarked.

Axel nodded. 'That's the difference between us,' he said. 'Your only concern is to relieve your conscience. You think the truth will set you free, that it will lift you to new heights. That you'll get back everything you had before this miserable business ever happened. But you never will. One of us has to consider the consequences. You're really incredibly selfish, Reilly, it's all about you and your scruples.'

'Actually I was thinking about Ingerid,' Reilly mumbled.

He let himself fall on to the sofa. His long hair cascaded forwards and concealed his face; only his big nose protruded from the tangled hair.

'I mean, she thinks it's her fault that Jon died, that she must have been a bad mum. This will haunt her for the rest of her life. She'll be thinking about it when she gets up and last thing at night before she falls asleep. And when she visits his grave, she'll think she was a bad mum who did everything wrong. And that's not true.'

'We all have bad stuff to deal with,' Axel said, his face contorting with pain. 'You've got to stop worrying about other people, Reilly, it restricts your ability to make the most of your life.'

'What do you think Jon wrote in that diary?' Reilly asked.

'Probably nothing revealing,' Axel said, 'or Ingerid would have been here a long time ago.'

'She won't come here,' Reilly declared. 'She'll go straight to the police. Do you know what I often think? They didn't believe our explanation for one minute. They've simply been waiting for something to surface. And that's happened now. They're ahead of us, Axel. They have been the whole time.'

Reilly's dark predictions sent Axel into a state of panic.

'I feel nauseous and limp,' he said, 'and I'm clammy. Do you think I've got blood poisoning?'

Reilly ignored the question. 'Someone might have seen us,' he said. 'I often think about that. We were so caught up in what happened that we wouldn't have noticed if someone had been watching us.'

Axel was still sitting with the flannel pressed against his cheek. He looked like a wounded soldier.

'Many people drown,' he said. 'It's probably not our guy.'

CHAPTER 19

The simplest and most obvious explanation is often the right one, Sejer thought. Jon jumped into the lake because he was ill. I've been doing this job for too long. I've developed a profound scepticism and it follows me everywhere. I don't trust anyone, I imagine that anything is possible, and I begin by assuming that he didn't drown himself. It's important to think like that. But it might be precisely what happened. Even if he couldn't swim, he might have managed to wade out into the water before he sank. He might have panicked and struggled with a strength he didn't know he possessed. His mortal struggle might have taken him further out. And even if he was planning on killing himself, he might have got dressed with just as much care as he always did, buttoned up his jacket, tied his shoelaces with double knots. There were no rules for what people might or might not do in such circumstances. He had heard numerous stories of bizarre behaviour before such an exit. Some tidied and put out the bin. Some dressed up and lit candles in the room where they were going to die. Some put on music, something to accompany them to the other side. Some took to the woods like old cats. And some took others with them when they went. Every life is unique, Sejer thought, and so is every death. He read the statements from Philip Reilly and Axel Frimann over and over. Something was wrong with their version of events. Frimann had seemed strangely unmoved despite the tragedy, and Reilly was very evasive. Yet he could see no motive for a crime. The three had known each other all their lives and Ingerid Moreno had vouched for both Philip and Axel. They had always looked after Jon like big brothers.

He sat listening to the hum of the police station. He liked being a part of a big engine. He liked interrogating people, he liked spotting the lie when it came. A lie had its own pitch, and over many years he had learned to recognise it. He liked the moment when the confession finally spilled out, when all the cards were on the table and the course of events could be mapped and filed. Your lawyer can now prepare a defence for you based on the information you have supplied. Give you what you are entitled to. Justice. Even understanding, possibly. And if there are mitigating circumstances, they will be taken into consideration. If you disagree with the verdict, you can appeal. And then you can appeal again.

He looked at his papers and noticed that Jon Moreno had gone to the cabin on Friday the 13th. An ominous date when anything could happen. How do I catch them, he speculated, and what do I actually charge them with?

He rolled his chair back from the desk and studied his legs. They were long and strong. They had always supported him. In the evenings he went running in the woods. He was healthy and tough; he had good stamina, he was fit. He leaned forward and placed his hands on his knees. He knew his legs were fine, they were not the source of the problem. The dizziness is in my head, he thought, I stumbled because something has happened up there.

The telephone rang. It was a relief to put his thoughts aside.

'I'm working on the man from Glitter Lake,' Snorrason said, 'and I'm sorry to say this, but so far I haven't been able to establish the cause of death. The length of time the body has spent in the water has made it difficult for us. It's badly decomposed. It was probably there the whole summer. Water washes away a lot of important information.'

'But you must have something,' Sejer asked hopefully.

A longish pause followed. Perhaps the forensic examiner was reading through his papers. Sejer scratched his elbow. As always his psoriasis flared up when something happened.

'I haven't found one piece of evidence to suggest that someone hurt him.'

'But he was dead when he ended up in the lake? You're sure about that?'

'I am.'

'That's enough evidence for me,' Sejer said. 'Dead people don't throw themselves into lakes. What about his identity? Tell me you know who he is.'

'The man's identity is clear and that's something at least,' Snorrason said contentedly. 'Or rather, the lad's, because he was only seventeen years old. He lived in Norway with his mother from the age of eight. They're from Vietnam. He disappeared in the middle of December and the circumstances surrounding his disappearance are unclear.'

'His name?' Sejer said.

'Van Chau,' Snorrason said. 'Kim Van Chau.'

'Could you repeat that, please?'

'Kim Van Chau,' Snorrason said.

Sejer noted it down on a pad. There was something familiar about that name and he racked his brains. Van Chau, he thought, Van Chau from Vietnam. Finally it surfaced in his memory, a missing person case from December, and the moment he remembered that, he caught a glimpse of something bigger, the breakthrough he had been waiting for and which had been there the whole time. Kim Van Chau had been reported missing after a party. After several extensive searches, they had given up on finding the young man. He seemed to have vanished without a trace. And Frimann, Reilly and Moreno had been involved. They had been brought in for routine questioning, but there had been no grounds for suspecting anything criminal. Now, many months later, his body had been found in Glitter Lake. Then another thought struck Sejer. His gaze swept across his desk to the rag doll with the blue overalls. Jon's doll from Ladegården, whose name was Kim.

CHAPTER 20

Dear diary,

I like everything here at Ladegården.

My room and my bed and Hanna Wigert. I like my medica-tion, which suppresses my anxiety. I like the structure and the routines, that there are always voices and sounds in the big building. I like the food we eat together at the long table in the dining hall. I like Dagny who works in the kitchen and Ruth, the night nurse, who looks in every hour during the night. The feeling of being cared for like a child. And perhaps that is what I am, a child still clinging to its mother's petticoats. At the same time being here is also tough because I realise now that there is no magic solution, no cure that will fix everything in a fortnight. They expect that I will work with them by opening up, by revealing my innermost thoughts. But if I do that I'll expose other people, and I don't feel that I have the right to do that. Should I save myself and let others go down? When I talk about these things to Hanna, it doesn't seem as though she under-stands the gravity. She says 'but you want to get through this, don't you, you want to change, don't you?' And, of course, I do because I can't live with myself. I'm Jon the Coward. I tell myself that over and over.

Jon the Coward, Jon the Coward, Jon the Coward.

Often when I wander up and down the corridor I am amazed that people smile and greet me as if I were a decent guy who deserves kindness. Can't they see that it's Jon the Coward? Don't they see the swarm of flies buzzing around my head? Don't they notice the trail of filth after me? So I walk on my own mostly or I go for walks with Molly. She is not like the others. She doesn't want to talk about things that are painful either, but I know she has an older brother whom she hates. She doesn't want to talk about him. She doesn't want to tell me his name, even, which makes me wonder what could have happened. Molly and I have become friends for life. We have never told each other, but we both know it, and when I see her, I feel all fizzy inside, like carbonated water. Yesterday I was in Hanna Wigert's office. I go there every day between eleven and twelve, and I sit on the blue sofa. I was holding one of the dolls in my lap as I always do. Sometimes I torture it a little. I pull its hair and pinch its feet, and it makes me feel better. I don't know if Hanna notices or if she understands why I do it, but I like torturing the doll. I have nowhere else to direct my rage. Towards the end of the session Hanna fell silent. She rolled her chair towards the sofa where I was sitting.

'What are you scared of, Jon?' she asked.

I got terribly agitated because I felt she was putting pressure on me, so I pulled the doll and the seams came apart. But I also wanted to be a good patient and give as much of an accurate and truthful answer as I could.

'Condemnation,' I whispered.

'Condemnation?'

She rolled even closer and she did not take her eyes off me.

'Who would condemn you?' she asked.

'People,' I said.

'People? All of them?'

'Yes. All of them.'

'Is your offence that great?'

'Yes, it's enormous.'

'Do you know every single person on the planet, Jon? Or just a few?'

'Just a few.'

'I see. A few. And you think they would condemn you?'

'Any decent person would,' I said.

'So you don't think there are any compassionate, understanding or forgiving people? Have you thought about it?'

'There aren't many of them,' I said. 'You'll condemn me too, you just don't know it yet.'

'You might be wrong,' she said.

'I'm not wrong. I might have been wrong on other occasions, most people have been. But this time I'm right.'

That was our conversation. After the session I felt wretched. Compassion? Forgiveness? We'll never get either of those. Not so long as we live.

I am on the horns of a dilemma. If I continue to keep my mouth shut then I'm a coward. And if I talk, Axel and Reilly will hate me.

CHAPTER 21

'What have you done?' Ingerid Moreno screamed.

She was standing in the door glaring at Axel, and she was incandescent with rage.

'Tell me what you did. Tell me now!'

Her cheeks were flushed as though she had been running and indeed she had been. She had run from the car to the block of flats where he lived, she had run from the lift to his door. She entered the room and slammed the door behind her. Her hair was standing straight up.

'Tell me what you did!'

Axel retreated. As usual his hand cupped his jaw. He paled at the sight of Ingerid Moreno. His brain worked frantically to catch up with the situation. He had anticipated that she might turn up, but he had expected a supplicant woman, not a fury.

'Answer me!' she screamed. 'I know that something happened, I've read Jon's diary. You did something and you're going to tell me what it was! And don't you dare lie to me, Axel, or I'll beat you senseless. And you can laugh at me, but you don't know how strong I am, I'll tear you to pieces if you don't give me an answer!'

Axel could not help but stare at her nails which were long and painted red. He forced his astonishment to the back of his mind, concentrated and finally regained the eloquence which always saved him.

'Ingerid,' he said gently. 'Come inside, please. Don't stand there screaming.'

He walked towards her with open arms, but she stepped back. In response he turned, crossed the floor and straightened up a little so his broad shoulders would come into full view. That way she would see that he was big, strong and self-assured, that it was he who decided what the truth was.

'Sit down,' he said kindly.

She perched on the edge of a chair. The red claws settled in her lap and she never once took her eyes off him.

'I'm sorry,' Axel said, 'but I've got an infected wisdom tooth, so I'm not quite myself. Ingerid, dear. You've got to explain what all this is about because I don't understand.'

Ingerid Moreno continued to stare at him. She might attack me at any time, Axel thought, she has lost Jon, she has nothing more to lose. She might claw out my eyes and people would understand. Poor Ingerid, they would say, she doesn't know what she's doing, she's mad with grief.

'I've read his diary,' she said. 'He wrote in it every single day and it's about you three. He writes that he has a guilty conscience, that the three of you did something dreadful, and if that was what killed him, then I have to know what it was!'

'The three of us did something?' he frowned.

He breathed with forced calm. But the rest of him was ready to strike. What do I do if we've been found out? he thought. I'll wring her neck. No, of course I won't. Damn you, Jon, for putting your guilty conscience on paper for everyone to see.

'He writes that we did something together?' he asked.

'Yes,' she said. 'The diary makes it quite clear. I didn't bring it with me, Axel, but there's no doubt. I knew Jon. He speaks as if a great sin was committed.'

'A great sin? And he's saying that Reilly and I were involved?'

He gave her a look of compassion, as you would look at an errant child. He was also trying to ignore the infernal pain from the wisdom tooth, which constantly threatened to knock him off balance.

'He doesn't say that in so many words,' she said, 'but he was only ever with you. He had no other friends.'

'He says we've done something dreadful, but he doesn't say what?' Axel whispered.

Ingerid bit her lip. She was finding it hard to sit still, she ached all over.

Axel had never seen her so agitated. Yet simultaneously he experienced a relief so tremendous that the agony from his tooth faded.

'Jon was ill,' he said softly.

His voice took on a comforting tone which made her listen.

'Do you hear, Ingerid? He was ill.'

Ingerid broke free from his hypnotic voice and turned sharp again. 'That diary was written in despair, not in madness. Don't underestimate me,' she snarled. 'Don't underestimate me because I'm a woman. Because I'm grieving. Because I'm older than you. Don't you dare do that!'

'You knew Jon,' Axel said calmly. 'You know what kind of conscience he had. He fretted about the slightest thing. Jon was a sensitive boy, his nerves forever fraying. I simply cannot imagine what could have tormented him to such an extent that he could not go on. There is nothing between us that can explain what happened. Perhaps he's referring to some trivial incident, something Reilly and I have long since forgotten, but which Jon brooded over. Perhaps it grew in magnitude and overwhelmed him. I'm so very sorry, Ingerid, but I don't understand a word of this.'

Ingerid Moreno was close to tears. She looked at Axel's face like a beggar. She had been so sure he had the answer.

'Please remember one thing,' Axel continued. 'Some people have a tendency to blow their sins and faults completely out of proportion. Tiny errors of judgement turn into monsters which consume them. That's probably what Jon did. It's called paranoia.'

Ingerid fought her tears. Axel's composure was beginning to make her have doubts.

'But there's something there,' she stuttered. 'Page after page about remorse. Page after page of self-loathing. I was so sure you would be able to help me. I'll go to Reilly now, I'll ask him.'

Axel gave her a compassionate look. 'I think you should. Do what you have to, but I'm afraid you'll be disappointed. Jon didn't do much wrong, I can assure you of that. Jon was sensitive and decent and upright. And though I know how hard it must be, you may have to accept that he could have been delusional.'

Ingerid got up and went to the door. 'Jon was nothing of the sort,' she said, 'I would have known about it. His doctor would have known. I'll unravel this somehow and if you're hiding something, I'll never forgive you!'

She started screaming again. She lost control, not that it was worth anything without Jon.

'I've known you since you were a little boy,' she shouted, 'and I know your mother. I've put plasters on your knees, made you toast and orange squash. You've come to my house for years and I've always thought well of you. You were a brat, but you were Jon's friend. And don't you dare deceive me now, I won't tolerate it!'

She slammed the door as she left. Axel grabbed his mobile and phoned Reilly.

'Are you awake?' he asked. 'Are you lucid? Ingerid Moreno will be with you in ten minutes.'

CHAPTER 22

Yoo Van Chau was a small woman with round childlike cheeks. When she saw Sejer, she spun around and buried her face in her hands. Some coats hung on one wall and she disappeared between a jacket and an overcoat. Sejer noticed two things. She had black silky hair and wore tiny embroidered slippers on her feet.

Having hidden behind the clothes for a while, she reappeared with an apologetic smile. He followed her into the living room and spotted a photo of Kim Van Chau straight away. It stood on a tall chest of drawers. A candle burned next to it. Kim was a handsome boy and he could not stop himself from thinking of the body they had dragged out of the water. It was not handsome, but Yoo Van Chau did not know that.

She gestured towards a sofa. It was red with golden trim. She sunk into a chair. Sejer could not take his eyes off the embroidered slippers. He thought he could make out a motif of fire-breathing dragons.

'I can make tea,' Yoo Van Chau said.

'Please don't trouble yourself,' Sejer said.

Her hands settled in her lap and a stream of words poured out of her. She spoke good Norwegian with a charming accent, and her voice was that of a little girl.

'They told me he was found close to the shore,' she said. 'That he's been lying there a long time. It's nine months now since he went missing. So I'm happy in a way. Because I had given up. I thought that all was lost and that my hands would be empty for ever.'

'Do you have any other children?' Sejer asked, hoping she would say yes. That any second now a teenage daughter would appear

110

from one of the rooms and put her arms around her mother's neck. Or a small child might crawl up into her lap. She seemed young.

'Kim's my only one,' she explained. 'We never had any more children, my husband died when he was only thirty-two. I couldn't support us on my own. Kim was only eight years old when we moved to Norway. We come from Yen Bai. We decided on Norway because we have family here and they said it was a fine country.'

'And what do you think?' Sejer asked. 'Is Norway a fine country?'

'You want for nothing,' she said simply.

Sejer did not reply.

'Kim didn't have many friends,' she went on. 'And whenever he found someone to spend time with, they wanted to go out drinking. That's what he said to me: if I want to hang out with them, I have to go drinking.'

She stopped her flow of words.

Sejer had listened in silence. To come all this way, he thought, from beautiful Vietnam, to the dark Norwegian winter with ice and snow and lose everything you have. And yet sit there calmly talking with your hands in your lap. Tiny porcelain hands. And fire-breathing dragons on your feet.

'Isn't it odd that some people end up without friends?' she said. 'After all, he wanted for nothing. He did well at school and you can see from the photo that he was good-looking, so it's hard for me to understand. It's very hard indeed.'

'Tell me about the night he went missing,' Sejer asked.

'Yes,' she said, 'I will tell you. It was 19 December last year, in the early evening. He wanted to go into town. He wasn't meeting anyone in particular, he just wanted to watch the world go by, he said, and I told him to dress up warm because it was freezing cold that day. And a seventeen-year-old boy should have some independence, I do know that, so I was happy that he wanted to go out and meet people even though I didn't know who they were. He called out to me from the hall. That was the last time I heard his voice, I can still hear his very last words. I went to bed at midnight, but I didn't go to sleep. I lay waiting for his key in the lock because it makes quite a loud noise, you can't mistake it. I listened out for his voice and his footsteps, and I waited for the pipes in the bathroom to gurgle. The night has never been so full of sounds. I kept hearing things, and every time I sat up with a start. Kim's coming, that's definitely Kim. Wasn't that the sound of a car starting in the road? They must have given him a lift home, after all he's gone out with nice people. Because he's a nice boy. That's what I thought as I lay in my bed. After several hours dawn broke and then I was sure that something must have happened. I stood in the doorway and looked at his empty bed. I could hardly believe it. Then there was the business of trying to find out what had happened. When he was reported missing in the newspaper, the police received some calls. It turned out he had met some young people and gone to a party with them, and they'd all been questioned, but none of them had any idea what might have happened to him. Kim had done what they had done. He had been drinking and he wasn't used to that. They made no bones about it. Kim was drunk. And I don't know what happened, but he shouldn't have been drinking because he can't handle it.'

'What do you think might have happened?' Sejer asked.

'For a long time I thought he might have fallen asleep in a ditch on his way home and frozen to death, but then I heard that he had been given a lift as far as the letterboxes and that's when I started to have doubts. But the days passed and no one found him, and I knew that this was something completely different, something incomprehensible. I don't understand why they found him in the water, perhaps he fell through the ice. But it was so cold last winter. The ice must have been thick, and what would he have been doing up at Glitter Lake?'

She wiped tears from her cheek. 'Are you sure you don't want some tea?' she asked again.

'Please don't trouble yourself,' Sejer said.

He regretted saying it immediately. Perhaps she would like

to go to the kitchen and do something, boil water, fetch cups from the cupboard, do the things she normally did when she had visitors. And he had rejected her hospitality. For a while he wondered if he should ask for a cup anyway, but he was too slow.

'Can you discover anything after such a long time?' she asked. 'I don't want to blame anyone, but if someone is responsible for what happened, then they must be punished for it. The police thought he might have killed himself because they soon found out that he was lonely, obviously. But Kim would never have done anything like that.'

'The case will be reopened,' Sejer said. 'Now that we've found him, it will be easier to investigate. He didn't drown, that much we do know, but the cause of his death is unknown. Was he in good health?'

She nodded. 'He was. He wasn't on medication, or anything. He didn't take drugs, I'm certain of it, and he didn't smoke, either.'

Again she started to weep softly. She straightened out an embroidered tablecloth and smiled apologetically for becoming emotional.

'If you discover the truth, I'll be happy,' she said. 'As it is now, I lie awake at night and imagine the very worst. What if they killed him? All the drunk young people at the party. What if they killed him?'

'They didn't,' Sejer said. 'The forensic examiner would have discovered that.'

'Is it possible to drink so much that it kills you?' she asked.

'Yes,' Sejer said, 'it is. And the forensic examiner has taken samples which will reveal whether he died from alcohol poisoning, but we don't think that's what happened.'

'Can you tell when people lie?' she asked.

He contemplated this for couple of seconds. 'Often, but not always.'

'Will you be speaking to the people who were with him that night?'

'I'll be speaking to every single one of them.'

Yoo Van Chau looked at him with piercing eyes.

'You must study everyone you talk to very closely,' she said. 'You must listen to their voices and look into their eyes to see if they speak the truth.'

'I'll listen very carefully to everything they've got to say,' Sejer said.

'And you must watch their hands,' she said. 'Observe what they do with their hands, if they flap.'

'I'll watch their hands,' he promised.

'Can you find out what happened?' she said, and now her voice was urgent. 'Will you know if anyone killed or tortured him? Can you find out why his heart stopped beating, his young, strong heart? There has to be a reason,' she pressed on. 'Nothing happens without a reason.'

'You're right about that,' he said, 'but you know, often several circumstances coincide.'

'Then I want to know all about those circumstances,' she said. 'Can you find them out? Please,' she added while she waited desperately for his reply. She looked small and lost in the big chair. Sejer did not want to promise her anything or give her any guarantees. He never did, he knew better than to do that. But suddenly he felt weak, and the forbidden words slipped out of him.

'I'll find out what happened,' he said. 'I promise.'

CHAPTER 23

The party had been held in Skjæret on 19 December. Skjæret was a town on the coast, near Åkerøy, and Irene Selmer was listed as the owner of a small flat with a terrace that overlooked the water.

They were walking to the car. Sejer confessed his brief moment of weakness when he was with Yoo Van Chau.

'I promised her I would find out,' he said.

'What do you mean promised?' Skarre said.

'That I would make sure she gets an explanation for it all. It was impossible to turn her down. She wears slippers embroidered with dragons,' he explained.

'But we can't promise her anything,' Skarre said, aghast. 'You need to use a stock phrase. We'll do everything in our power. That one is quite good. It makes an impression, don't you think?'

'If you had seen Yoo Van Chau, you would have made promises too,' Sejer said.

They drove out to Åkerøy.

Half an hour later they saw the fjord sparkle blue between the houses. Small islands dotted with red and white cottages lay beyond. Skarre spoke at length about his childhood. He had grown up in a vicarage on the south coast, and he could feel the pull of it now.

'I want a flat out here,' he said. 'How much do you think they cost?'

'Far too much for us,' Sejer replied.

Skarre stared dreamily across the mouth of the fjord.

'I suppose it gets cold here in the autumn and winter,' he added. 'After all, it's right on the coast. What do you think?'

He looked to the inspector for support.

'You can't live out here,' Sejer said. 'It's freezing cold.'

Irene Selmer was wearing a T-shirt which came down to her thighs and read: PRINCESS ON A BINGE. She acted curt. She seemed to think they might be selling something, and she wanted shot of them.

'Police,' Sejer said.

She gawped. Then she recalled what had happened. It had upset her.

'Is it Jon Moreno?'

Sejer did not have time to answer.

'I heard he killed himself,' she said. 'Did he?'

'We're here on another matter,' Sejer said.

She tugged at her T-shirt. She showed no sign of inviting them in. Then another unpleasant thought occurred to her, something she had almost forgotten.

'We've found Kim Van Chau,' Sejer said.

'Is he dead?' she whispered.

'Yes.'

'Did he freeze to death? Where was he?'

'We found him in Glitter Lake,' Skarre explained.

She shook her head, baffled. 'Glitter Lake? But he lives in Nattmål, in those terraced houses. Do you know what happened?'

'No,' Skarre said, looking at Sejer. 'But we'll do everything in our power to find out.'

She turned around and went back inside the flat.

'I shouldn't have thrown him out,' she said. 'He was so drunk. It's all my fault.'

'Why is it your fault?' Sejer asked.

Without looking at them she began to explain. 'If I had let him stay the night, he would have got home alive. But I didn't want him here. I don't know what I was thinking.'

'Let's begin at the beginning,' Sejer said. 'We can apportion blame later.'

They all sat down. Irene Selmer lifted the edge of her T-shirt and wiped her eyes, causing her black make-up to smudge.

'I've given a statement,' she said. 'I've told you what happened several times already.'

'And now you need to tell me again,' Sejer said. 'Tell us about the party.'

'It was a house-warming party,' she said. 'My dad gave me this flat when I turned twenty. It was quite low-key. We sat on the floor because there weren't enough chairs for everybody. I'd warned all the neighbours, these walls are so thin. But no one complained because everyone who lives out here is young, and they don't mind. We ordered pizzas from Pizzabussen, they were delivered at ten.'

'Did people get very drunk?' Sejer asked.

She tugged at her shoelaces.

'People wanted to get drunk. Some had brought beer and wine, others vodka. Of course people got drunk, I had expected them to.'

'How did you know Kim Van Chau?' Skarre asked.

'I didn't know Kim. He wasn't invited.'

'So tell us how he ended up at your party.'

'He was hitch-hiking,' she said. 'From Nattmål. He wanted to go into town. Two friends of mine drove past on their way here and spotted him. And they invited him to come along. They just did it for a laugh.'

She jerked her head involuntarily. Perhaps she was ashamed or perhaps she had just had enough.

'He sat down on the floor,' she said, 'and someone handed him a bottle of beer. And then another and another. He couldn't hold his drink. We made him speak Vietnamese. It sounded so funny. Every time we started laughing, so did he. He did everything we asked him to.'

'Did he tell you anything about himself?'

She thought about it.

'He lived with his mum in one of those terraced housed in Nattmål. And he went to Sanderud College. His dad is dead. That was all we knew.'

She looked up at Sejer.

'He had a bottle in his hand the whole time,' she said, 'and I told them they had to stop it because we didn't even know if he was allowed to drink alcohol. And he still had to get home. Somehow or other.'

'And that was how the evening went on? You sat on the floor drinking?'

'As you can see, there's not enough room to dance here,' she said.

'Go on,' Sejer said. 'What happened next?'

'It was late,' she said, 'and I had to throw people out because no one wanted to leave. It was so cold outside. It's impossible to have a conversation with drunk people,' she sighed.

Sejer looked at her gravely.

'Was there anything else, apart from alcohol, being passed around that night?'

'Not that I know of. And if I had suspected anything, then I would have made people stop. I can't risk it. My dad would kill me.'

'Do you like Axel Frimann?' Skarre asked.

She looked confused. 'He's always got loads of girls chasing after him.'

'Strictly speaking that's not a proper answer to my question,' Skarre said.

'Being Axel's girl gives you status,' she explained.

'I understand he's quite a guy,' Skarre said.

'I don't care about status,' she said.

'You started throwing people out,' Sejer said. 'How did they get home?'

'Most of them took a cab. They shared and split the fare. Some walked because they live locally, and a few had caught the last bus.'

'And Kim Van Chau?'

'He was the biggest problem. At that point he was really drunk. But it was three o'clock by then, and I didn't want anyone sleeping on the floor when I woke up in the morning. He didn't have any money either, so I told Axel and the others that they had to give him a lift back. They could drop him right where my friends had picked him up, right by the letterboxes at the bottom of the hill in Nattmål. From there it's only a short walk to his front door. I thought about his mum, she was probably waiting up for him. Then we had a row.'

'And what was the outcome?' Sejer asked.

'It ended up that Axel and Reilly dragged him through the door and bundled him into the Mercedes,' she said. 'But that was after I had argued with Axel for a long time. He is very stubborn.'

'Had Axel been drinking?'

'Don't think so,' she mumbled. She started twirling a ring on her finger and Sejer recalled Yoo Van Chau's words. Watch their hands, see if they flap.

'What about Reilly and Jon?'

'Jon was completely out of it,' Irene said, 'because he couldn't hold his drink either. And Reilly was looking pretty wasted, too.'

'So we have the following scenario,' Sejer said. 'It's three o'clock in the morning. Axel, Jon, Reilly and Kim leave by the front door to drive to Nattmål. Did you see them get into the car?'

'I can only see the water,' she said.

'But as far as you were concerned, Axel was driving Kim to Nattmål?'

'That was the deal,' she said. 'He promised. Jon and Reilly promised.'

'So that was the last time you saw Kim Van Chau?' Sejer asked. 'When Axel and Reilly helped him through the door?'

'Yes,' she said. 'That was the last time I saw him.'

CHAPTER 24

Ingar and Ragni Lund had also been to Irene's party in Skjæret. They were twins. Sejer was fascinated by their similarities, which manifested themselves not only in their features, but also in their gestures, even though they were not identical twins.

'When we turned up, the party had already been going for a couple of hours,' Ragni explained, 'and Kim had been assigned the role of mascot.'

'He was drunk. He laughed at everything we said. He looked like a happy little goblin with his black hair.'

Sejer made a note and looked up at the twins again.

'Did anyone leave the party and come back later?' he wanted to know.

'Yes, someone did, didn't they? Stian and Jon went off to buy mixers,' Ingar said. 'There's a petrol station on the main road which is always open. Shell,' he explained. 'They were gone about half an hour.'

'Anyone else?'

'No.'

'Did anyone go into the other rooms?'

They both shook their heads.

'Irene had locked the door to her bedroom,' Ragni explained, 'because she didn't want anyone making out in there.'

'Do you know if any of the guests already knew Kim?'

'No one knew Kim,' Ragni said. 'Suddenly he appeared in the doorway, and Irene didn't have the heart to tell him to go. It was so cold that night, it was almost minus twenty, and he wasn't properly dressed. He was only wearing a thin jacket. He wouldn't have survived.' And then she remembered that he had not survived.

'Were there any problems during the evening?'

'Only minor rows,' Ingar said.

'About what?'

'Boys' stuff. When did bass player X leave band Y, and who took over from him and when did he OD and so on. The kind of things that boys are into.'

'No arguments relating to Kim?'

'No.'

'No form of harassment or bullying?'

The twins shook their heads. 'We were messing about about, but it was nothing serious.'

'Would you say that Jon Moreno was drunk?' Sejer asked.

'Yes,' Ingar said. 'He was drunk.'

'And Philip Reilly?'

'He was quite wasted, but he's bigger, so he can handle more.'

'What about Axel Frimann?'

'I think he'd had a few beers earlier in the evening,' Ragni said, 'but he was driving so he was careful. He's fanatical when it comes to that Mercedes. He would never take any chances with it.'

'When did you leave the party?'

'Round about one o'clock,' Ingar said. 'I think we were among the first to leave. We caught the last bus into town.'

Sejer put down his pen.

'Kim was found in Glitter Lake,' he said. 'Do you know of a place there where young people tend to meet? A beach, a view-point?'

'There's a beach we go to. We have a lot of parties there in the summer. You drive up along the west side,' Ragni explained, 'past the asylum seekers' centre, and then you take a sharp right. It's a tiny beach. We call it Copacabana.'

CHAPTER 25

Yoo Van Chau put on a knitted jacket and boots to go down to the letterboxes. At the bottom of the road she stopped and shivered while she pondered that this was the very spot where Kim had stood alone in the cold, hitch-hiking, and a car had pulled over. I imagine he must have been thrilled to be invited to a party, she thought. Finally someone had noticed him and included him. Everything he had always dreamed of had rolled up on four wheels. Two pretty girls and an invitation. Hey you, do you want to come with us? For a moment she was so stunned that she temporarily forgot why she had left the house. She opened her letterbox. Inside lay a thick pile of junk mail. For coffins. And headstones. There was also a catalogue from a florist. Even death is a business, she thought; they get you when you're down. There are probably some greedy people behind all this glossy paper. Then she remembered that they too would die, the people who made the coffins and carved the stones. And those who tied the wreaths. Sons would die and daughters, mothers would die and fathers, every single one of them would have to make these choices. She felt limp. She clung to the letterbox for a moment and the catalogues slipped from her hands and on to the ground. She had to squat down to pick them up. She sat there clawing at the coffins and the flowers and the headstones. Some dirt had got on to the pages. She wiped it off with her sleeve.

Then she returned to the terraced houses. She walked quickly because she did not want to talk to anyone or explain herself. She went back inside, closed the door behind her and left the catalogues on the table. I will look at them, she thought, but not right now. I need something to eat. I need a cup of tea. And then I need to rest because it's a big decision. I need to be calm and rested, not flustered and distressed. She went into the kitchen and found a loaf in the bread bin, some butter and jam in the fridge. He came home, she thought, just as I had given up hope. I suppose I should be pleased about that because it's much more than I had last winter. Then I had only words and suggestions from people I'd never met, and no one would take the blame for anything. What had they done apart from opening their door to him? She did not think that anyone had hurt him. Why would they? He was not aggressive. She leaned over the kitchen counter with her thoughts. She could not comprehend why she had lost him, why he had been found floating in Glitter Lake.

She made a jam sandwich and a cup of tea and carried them into the living room. There she ate her modest meal, never once taking her eyes off the catalogues. I'll go through them, she thought, but first I need to rest. I'm so tired. I'm exhausted. She pulled a blanket over herself and curled up on the sofa where she dozed. Music, she thought. Flowers. Kim in a box on the floor. They called it a coffin and it was decorated both inside and out, almost like a nest with lining and ruches, but it was still just a box. She placed a hand on her heart. It beat softly under her blouse as though nothing had happened, unaffected by the violent pain she felt in this precise muscle.

She lay very still for an hour. She kept wanting to get up and do something, but she could not summon the energy. She listened to the sounds from outside, people coming and going in the street. Out there people were busy, as always, it was only her world which had been shattered. I could die now, she thought, and no one would find me. I could lie here for weeks until someone noticed a smell outside my front door. The thought of this made her leap up. I need to pull myself together, she thought, I have things to arrange for Kim, I can't lie here doing nothing. She folded the blanket and took the first catalogue from the pile. Feeling nervous, she sat down and started going through it. She ticked the headstones she liked best, but no matter what they looked like, they were terribly expensive. She had no idea they would cost so much. But then again someone had spent time chipping, carving and polishing. It was craftsmanship; of course it cost money.

She put down the catalogue and picked up another. She realised she was looking for something she would never find. She wanted something simple; they were simple people. But she also wanted the stone to stand out from the others in the cemetery because there was only one Kim. She reclined and closed her eyes, but her whole body was tense. She leaned forward to get a new catalogue. There was only one coffin she liked. It was mahogany and way beyond her means. She kept staring at the picture. She liked the dark wood. She was upset that she could not afford it. Again she put the catalogue aside. Another thought had distracted her. She had to find some pall-bearers, some boys from his class, perhaps. She would have to talk to Kim's teacher, he would probably organise it for her if she asked him nicely. They had never wanted to be with him when he was alive, but now they would have to do him a final favour whether they wanted to or not, she decided.

Afterwards she probably ought to hold a small wake. But where? She didn't have enough room here. She would have to organise some refreshments too, and she would have to take the young people into consideration; after all they don't eat just anything, she thought. What will he wear, she wondered? This question unsettled her because it was important, and she had not given it a single thought. She did not want him in a white shroud. Kim would have hated that, but nor did he own a dark suit. So she would have to buy one. She knew his size; he was her son. A dark suit and a snow white shirt. Stylish, elegant and dignified. Then a dreadful thought struck her. It had lain dormant inside her for a long time, but she had pushed it aside. Kim had been in the water for many months. It would quite simply be impossible to dress him.

CHAPTER 26

Reilly had been well prepared, but now all his preparations went out of the window.

'You've found that Vietnamese guy,' he said. 'I suppose that's why you're here?'

'Correct,' Sejer said. 'We've found him.'

Reilly tried to arrange his gangly body, but it was not until he picked up the kitten that he settled down. He had anticipated a barrage of questions, but they just watched him in silence.

'I expect you've read the statement I gave last winter, and now you want me to repeat that and it's fine, I suppose, you have certain procedures and I understand that. The problem is that statement still stands. I presume that you've read it.'

He had to draw breath. He picked nervously at his corduroy trousers. They were slightly too big for him and shone with wear across the knees.

'No,' Sejer said. 'We haven't read it.'

This white lie baffled Reilly. 'You haven't?'

'I don't like to be prejudiced,' Sejer said. 'I prefer to draw my own conclusions. And Skarre wants to make his own notes.'

Reilly was not entirely sure if he was being serious. He started pacing up and down with the kitten in his arms. It dug its claws into his jumper, terrified of falling from a great height. What do they want from me? he thought, as he wandered around. How do you act if you've got nothing to hide? You sit down, look them in the eye. You smile a friendly and open smile. But he could not manage a smile, and he did have something to hide.

'How did he die?' he asked.

The two police officers were sitting down on the sofa. He noticed that Skarre had started making notes.

'It's difficult to establish the cause of death after such a long time,' Sejer said. 'And it's especially difficult when the body is found in water. We found him in Glitter Lake.'

Reilly started talking again even though Axel had advised him not to. Just answer their questions, he had said, otherwise keep your mouth shut. Your head's never straight, either, don't get yourself into trouble.

'We were only trying to help,' he said. 'No one else in Skjæret would take responsibility for him. Irene was dead set on getting rid of him. She was adamant that no one was allowed to stay the night, and that girl is a bit of a bitch. She had even locked the door to her bedroom. But if a poor little guy like him had slept in a corner, what harm would it have done? Not that I'm blaming Irene,' he said quickly. 'That's not how I meant it.'

'It wasn't easy to get him out of the flat either,' he carried on. 'It was like trying to get jelly to walk.'

'What time was it when you got to Nattmål?' Sejer asked.

'It must have been close to three-thirty because we left the party at three,' Reilly said, 'and we drove straight there. But it was snowing, so we drove slowly. Axel takes no chances with his Mercedes, he's terrified of denting it. It's quite an expensive model,' he added, 'with leather seats and all sorts of gadgets.'

'Now that he has been found dead,' Sejer said, 'what are your thoughts? Do you feel guilty?'

Reilly straightened up and glared down at them.

'Do I feel guilty?'

Frustrated, he tossed his long hair. The kitten was startled by the sudden movement.

'Of course I feel guilty. I feel guilty that we didn't walk him to his front door. Perhaps we should have helped him unlock it, and perhaps we should have put him to bed too. That's what you mean, isn't it?'

He turned his back to them. Aimlessly, he rearranged some small pots on the windowsill.

'Jon was also troubled by guilt,' Sejer said. 'It's clear from his diary, which we've been studying in detail. But there's something about his sense of guilt which disturbs us. We can understand that you've gone a few rounds with yourselves and from time to time felt a certain responsibility for what happened. But based on what you've just described, it's hard to understand why Jon would choose to end his life. That decision is not in proportion with your story.'

Reilly resumed his pacing. 'Oh yes,' he said. 'It fits perfectly, but you didn't know Jon. He believed everything rested with us. That we shouldn't have left him in the street. But I think that's excessive. No one else would take him. At least we brought him home. We dropped him off by the letterboxes at the bottom of the hill. When we left he was heading for the houses. A little unsteady on his feet, of course, but he was walking. The next day we learned that he had gone missing. We didn't understand how that was possible.'

'Was there any traffic in the area?'

'The odd car.'

'Did you talk to him when you dropped him off?'

Reilly nodded. 'We told him to go to bed. We asked if he had a key, and he said yes, he had a key in his pocket. We were tired and we wanted to go home, so we turned the car around and drove off. That's all I've got to say. I've told you this so many times, and I don't know any more than you do. By the way, having this hang over your head month after month is actually very stressful,' he said, 'and I don't mind admitting that I would like to put the whole mess behind me.'

'I can understand that,' Sejer said, 'but it has only just started.'

After interviewing Philip Reilly, Sejer and Skarre drove up to Glitter Lake. They passed the asylum seekers' centre. In front of the low, barrack-like building a number of men were wandering about. A couple of them sat on a bench smoking. Others were tossing a basketball into a hoop.

'Two brothers from Gambia drowned here last year,' Skarre said. 'Do you remember? They were eight and eleven. Their mother still lives at the detention centre. She never goes outside.'

'I do remember,' Sejer said. 'It was last May. The water was cold.'

Shortly afterwards they turned right and immediately spotted the beach, which had a small hill beside it. Scrub grew around it like a dense wreath, and some of the vegetation overhung the water. Sejer started climbing and soon reached the highest point.

From there he could see the small jetty from which the Gambian boys had gone swimming. He could also see the whirlpool where Kim Van Chau had been found. On the other side of the water lay two or three wooden cabins. There was a bright reflection from a window. Something black scurried past a wall, a dog presumably. He imagined being able to hear his way to the crime, that shouts and screams still lingered in the air – if there had been shouting and screaming – and that he would be able to detect them if he concentrated hard enough. The energy must still be here, he thought, and the fear. The rage. Or despair, that is what makes us kill, and they might have killed him, perhaps to conceal another crime. Or to cover up a mistake. But what kind of mistake? How much can go wrong in a warm Mercedes driving from Skjæret to Nattmål? He looked down at Skarre. He appeared to be listening too. From time to time he would squat and dig his fingers into the coarse sand. Sejer climbed down from the hill.

'Copacabana,' Skarre said. 'What do you think happened?'

Sejer thought about Philip Reilly, who had expressed so many contradictory feelings. Bitterness, despair and guilt. His explanation was unlikely to be true, but it was characterised by a form of righteous indignation, as if something external had taken control of their lives and they could not be held to account for that. Then he thought, Jon Moreno is dead. Reilly is the weakest link now. And he knows it.

'They drove here,' he said.

'But why?' Skarre asked.

'Because something went wrong and they had to cover it up.'

'Perhaps something had already happened at the party,' Skarre suggested. 'And they're protecting each other.'

'In that case there would be an awful lot of people who would need to keep their mouths shut for a very long time,' Sejer said. 'Someone is directly responsible for the situation that arose. They didn't contact the emergency services. They agreed a story and they've all stuck to it. Reilly, Frimann and Moreno were tasked with disposing of the body because they had access to a car. That could have been what happened.'

He started walking back to the car. Skarre followed him slowly. When they were both back inside, Sejer sat silently with his hands on the wheel. He stayed like that for a long time, pondering. Skarre noticed how grey he had become and how he had grown leaner and more lined over the years. On his right hand he wore his late wife's wedding ring. He had had it melted down with his own. He might be thinking about her now or maybe about the older man in the mirror who stared back at him each morning. Or perhaps he was thinking about Yoo Van Chau and the promise he had made her.

'You're bloody brilliant, but you can't crack them all,' Skarre said.

There was no reply. Sejer was lost in his own thoughts.

'What I'm saying is that you're only human,' Skarre went on. 'If you have to break your promise to Yoo Van Chau, it doesn't necessarily follow that you have failed or that you haven't met your own high standards. Do you lie awake at night, Konrad?'

'Axel Frimann's Mercedes,' Sejer said. 'I want it sent to forensics right now.'

Ingerid Moreno was an attractive woman, but grief had ravaged her. Her cheeks were sunken and her fingers were feeble when she buttoned her coat. It was late October. She tied a floral shawl around her neck. She had decided to take action. Passively grieving or waiting for something that might never happen was making her ill. But it was hard for her to move. Her body was weighed down by lethargy, and the things she had done automatically, such as getting dressed, locking the front door and going to her car, took much longer than usual. She was used to her days being familiar, predictable entities, like a staircase she would walk up every morning and find her bed at the top. The staircase had collapsed now. It had been reduced to rubble and she did not know how to climb it.

The wind caught her shawl as she reached the flagstone path. It was a colourful shawl decorated with red poppies that she had bought in Naples. It was there she had met Tony Moreno. She got in her car and drove to Nattmål. She stopped at the foot of the hill and thought for a while. Then she got out to check the letterboxes to make sure she was in the right place. Do I dare, she wondered, have I really got the nerve? I have no right. Nevertheless she drove up the long hill until she reached the terraced houses. She stayed in her car listening to a piece of music on the radio. When it has finished, I'll go in, she decided. A few minutes later she headed for Yoo Van Chau's front door. Suddenly she was on the verge of tears. She had no idea what might happen to her. A furious woman might appear at the door, screaming, don't come near me with your grief, I've got enough with my own. She heard a faint click from the lock. A tiny dark-haired woman gave her a quizzical look and Ingerid felt enormous and clumsy.

'You don't know me,' she stuttered, 'but I know who you are. I read about your son in the papers. About Kim.'

She wanted to hurry up and explain herself. She did not know how long the other woman would be prepared to listen.

'I've lost my son too,' she said. 'He drowned himself. Or at least we think he did, but it's not certain. There's something very strange going on which we don't understand. It happened just a few weeks ago. He was on a trip with some friends, and when they woke up in the morning he was gone. That's what they said. The police came to my house yesterday,' she said. 'They told me something new and I got really scared.'

She grew more animated because Yoo Van Chau did not look as if she was about to stop her.

'He went to the same party, in December. Out at Skjæret, near Åkerøy. He was there with Kim.'

Total silence followed. Yoo made a move towards Ingerid and placed a hand on her arm. Her eyes were huge and shining.

'Now they're both dead,' Ingerid said. 'Do you understand what happened at that party?'

'Please come in,' Yoo said. She stepped aside; the hallway was narrow. The moment they entered the living room Ingerid spotted the photograph on the chest of drawers. For a while she studied the young Vietnamese man.

'You've lost a handsome boy,' she said.

Yoo placed a hand on her heart. She would keep all the beautiful words spoken about Kim in there and carry them with her.

'Jon was very fair,' Ingerid said. 'But he was also slender, and he was the smallest. Of the three of them,' she explained. 'You know, Axel and Reilly. Have you met Axel and Reilly? His friends?'

'No,' Yoo said. 'I haven't met them. But they were the ones who gave Kim a lift home. They drove him as far as the letterboxes. That's what they told the police. I don't know if that's true. I don't know anything any more.' Suddenly a thought occurred to her. 'Was your son in that car?'

'Yes,' Ingerid said. 'He was in the car.' She felt utterly desolate. Now that they had arrived at the unpleasant part, the incident she was still unclear about, her strength deserted her. 'Please may I sit down?'

Yoo gestured towards the sofa. She slipped into an armchair with an elegance which reminded Ingerid of a swan gliding on water.

'I don't know what happened,' Ingerid said. 'I don't know what Jon was mixed up in, and I can barely look you in the eye, but I have to. It pains me to think that Jon might have done something illegal. He was a decent lad. He knew the difference between right and wrong, I'm absolutely convinced of that, but there were several of them in the car that night, and they had been drinking. Jon died in the middle of September,' she said. 'He was found at the bottom of the lake they call Dead Water.'

'Dead Water?' Yoo said.

'Your son was found in a lake too,' Ingerid said. 'It all means something. I believe that now.'

She was starting to become distressed and had to compose herself.

'Jon left behind a diary,' she said. 'He writes page after page about how guilty he feels. That he doesn't deserve to live. I think it has to do with Kim. That's why I wanted to meet you. We have to find out what happened that night.'

Yoo listened quietly. She had a serenity which made Ingerid relax her shoulders.

'Jon was in hospital,' she explained. 'He had had a nervous breakdown. But he never mentioned that he was planning to kill himself, and I still find it hard to believe. When someone commits suicide, strong forces are involved. But did they really come from inside him? Or was it something external that killed him? This is what troubles me.'

'Kim got into a car,' Yoo said, 'because he wanted to go to a party. There were two girls in it. I wonder who they were and what they were thinking when they saw him standing by the side of the road. I was sitting in this chair as they drove off. I should have taken better care of him.'

'You can't babysit a seventeen-year-old,' Ingerid said. 'They're off on their own. They get mixed up in things. Surely that's not our fault?'

'That's not our fault,' Yoo agreed.

They looked each other in the eye.

'But I'm still convinced that someone out there is guilty of something, and I want that guilt apportioned,' Ingerid said.

'What are we going to do?' Yoo whispered.

Ingerid gave her a triumphant look. 'Jon's friends, Axel and Reilly. They're hiding something. In Jon's diary it's clear that something happened, something got out of control. Do you follow? Something is going on behind our backs.'

Yoo leaned forward in her armchair, listening.

'What scares me the most,' Ingerid said, 'is that the police won't be able to arrest them. Because it gets harder after such a long period of time and because they haven't found any evidence, you know, as Kim was in the water for so long. But I can't bear doing nothing, I have to do something. We can't beat them up, but we can scare the living daylights out of them.'

Yoo Van Chau was thrilled to have found someone who felt the same way.

'I'm thinking of inventing a lie,' Ingerid said. 'Give them a taste of their own medicine. I want to give them a wake-up call.'

'A wake-up call?'

'An anonymous letter,' Ingerid said, 'which will make them think that someone is on to them. That's what they're scared of, isn't it, that someone suspects them? You do and I do, and I want them to know that.'

Yoo clenched her fists in her lap; her cheeks were flushed. 'We'll write a letter,' she said, 'but you need to write it. I make so many mistakes. Speaking Norwegian is no problem but writing it is difficult. I'll get some paper.'

Yoo leapt up from her chair and went over to the chest of drawers where Kim's photograph stood. Suddenly she waved her fist in the air. 'We'll get them,' she said.

She opened one of the drawers and rummaged around. Then she returned with pen and paper. Ingerid took them.

'It must be short,' she said, 'and to the point. It must be menacing.'

Yoo felt vengeance fill her heart, and it was true what they said: revenge was sweet. Ingerid started scribbling. She crossed her scrawl out and wrote something else. Yoo looked like a child expecting an exciting present. She perched on the edge of her armchair and craned her neck. Ingerid crossed her words out again, frowned and tore off the sheet. Eventually she frowned with determination and wrote without hesitation. Then she pushed the pad across the coffee table.

WE KNOW WHAT YOU DID.
WE ARE WATCHING YOU.

'Where do we send it?' Yoo asked.
'To Reilly,' Ingerid said. 'Reilly is weaker.'

Afterwards Yoo retrieved an atlas from the bookcase.

She pointed as she explained to Ingerid, 'Look, that's China, Laos and Cambodia. Here's the South China Sea and the Gulf of Thailand. And this', she said, 'is Vietnam.'

The small country was reproduced in purple. North-west of Hanoi lay the town of Yen Bai. She drew a long line with the tip of her finger up to Norway.

'We had to leave it all behind,' she said, 'when my husband got sick and died, and we were all alone.'

Then Ingerid pointed to Italy, which was reproduced in pink. She placed her finger on Naples.

'Jon's father lives here,' she explained. 'He left when Jon was a little boy. One day he just packed his bags and vanished. Then there was only Jon and me.'

Yoo put the atlas away.

'Our sons are dead,' Ingerid said, 'but we're not. I want to go outside in the wind. Do you have some stale bread so we can feed the ducks? Put on a warm coat.'

Yoo quickly went to the kitchen to fetch some bread. When they got outside they were hit by an icy blast.

'As if grief weren't bad enough,' Ingerid said, 'the gods have sent us a storm.'

They clung to each other as they walked. No one else had ventured out in the cold weather. It took them half an hour to walk to the pond. They found a bench by the water's edge and Yoo took the bag of bread from her handbag. The ducks heard the rustling and zoomed in on them like small ships in a dense feather-clad fan formation. Their orange feet paddled energetically in the water.

'It doesn't matter if we get a bit chilly,' Ingerid said. 'We can warm up afterwards. How are you doing? Are your hands freezing?'

Yoo started tossing pieces of bread at the ducks. She found it amusing the way they all made a beeline for her. It seemed like devotion.

'I'm going to come here every day,' she vowed. 'With stale bread.'

'I would like to come with you,' Ingerid said. 'If you don't mind.' She gave the small woman a kind look.

'Do you know what I often think?' Ingerid said. 'When something terrible happens, we talk about people getting over it. Is she over it? we say, as if the tragedy is an obstacle in someone's path and we have to scale it. It's not that straightforward. Grieving is something we have to live with,' she said, 'it's a constant battle. And the enemy is the rest of our lives. All those nights. All those hours.'

She was reminded of something she had read in Jon's diary. 'He was so horribly ashamed,' she explained. 'He was so burdened by guilt and shame. He wrote as though he didn't deserve to live.'

Ingerid looked down at the bread that Yoo was holding in her hand.

'That crust of bread reminds me of something,' she said. 'A man was in a German prison camp during the war. He was subjected to so many awful things – abuse, torture, starvation and exposure. There were thirty men crammed into a freezing barrack, and the snow blew in under the door. Nevertheless he survived, and when the war ended he returned home. Though he now had plenty of food and warmth, he died shortly afterwards. He was haunted by a terrible memory. One night he had stolen a crust of bread from a sleeping man. It was this incident that killed him. He could not bear to eat.'

'That's very sad,' Yoo said. She could visualise it all, an emaciated man in prison clothes stealing in the night. Crouching alone in the dark, furtively gnawing at the dry crust.

'That's one way of looking at it,' Ingerid said. 'But I also think that it says something positive about people. We need a sense of decency. Without it we cannot live a good life. And Jon had lost that sense of decency.'

Yoo looked down at what was left of the crust.

Ingerid took one of her hands and gave it a friendly squeeze.

'Put your gloves back on,' she ordered her. 'You're freezing. Look. They want more.' She pointed to the ducks, which kept coming.

'I think we've made friends for life,' Yoo smiled.

Afterwards they headed towards Nattmål to warm up with a pot of tea.

'Kim is never coming home again,' Yoo said. 'That means that no one will find me when I die. Not for a long time. Not many people come to my house,' she explained.

'That could happen to me too,' Ingerid said. 'I have an idea. Why don't we call each other every evening?'

At that Yoo looped her arm though Ingerid's, and they walked the last stretch close together.

'What about us?' she remembered when they were back inside. 'Is sending that letter to Reilly an act of decency?'

Ingerid had her answer ready.

'We forgive the poor wretch who stole the bread,' she said. 'He stole because he was in need. And so are we. Different rules apply.'

CHAPTER 29

Axel Frimann was speechless when Reilly told him about the letter and his silence lasted for quite some time. Reilly pressed his mobile to his ear. He could clearly visualise Axel's jaw muscles twitching as he reacted to the news.

'Bloody hell,' he heard.

And he repeated the oath with more emphasis.

'Bloody hell.'

While he waited for Axel to continue, Reilly wandered around the flat in circles. The kitten chased him and clawed at his trouser leg.

'Jon has exposed us,' Axel said.

'Never,' Reilly said.

'Who else could it be?' Axel said. 'Use your head, man!'

Reilly carried on wandering; the kitten carried on stalking him.

'Posted locally?' Axel asked.

'Yes. Nice envelope. Nice paper and pen. Capital letters.'

'Nice paper? A girl's behind it,' Axel declared. 'It's got to be Molly.'

'But it says "we",' Reilly reminded him. '"We know what you did."'

Axel fell silent again and Reilly wondered if he, too, was walking around his flat but in larger circles, as his living room was three times bigger.

'I think we may have to go away for a while,' he heard Axel say.

Reilly stopped pacing. From where he was standing, he could see the letter lying on the table, shiny and white.

'I have work,' he said. 'I can't go away.'

'For a couple of days, I mean,' Axel said. 'We'll go this Friday.

You've got the weekend off, haven't you? We'll go up to Dead Water. We need a break. And we need to discuss some important stuff. There's a lot at stake. Wouldn't you agree?'

Reilly stared out at the autumn weather. The wind was rising and the treetops outside his window were swaying.

'I'll buy some delicious food,' Axel tempted him. His voice was enticing. He wanted to enforce his will. 'I'll pick you up around six,' he added. 'Reilly, are you listening?'

'But why are we running away?' Reilly asked. 'Someone saw us. They're watching our every move. It's only a matter of time before they come knocking on my door.'

'Everything is a matter of time,' Axel said. 'The world will end, it's only a matter of time. You and I are going to die, it's only a matter of time. We've made it this far and we'll manage the rest.'

Reilly finally agreed to a weekend at the cabin. For years now he had allowed himself to be controlled by Axel's strong will. When the conversation was over, he sat in his chair for a long time with the kitten on his lap. He took some GHB, but it failed to calm him, so he took some more, and then he grew agitated. He was starting to have doubts. Why did Axel want to go to Dead Water? What were his motives? He glanced at the letter again.

We are watching you. How? he wondered. Were they following him in the street? Were they waiting outside the hospital when he turned up for work? Were they hiding behind the screens in the corridors watching all his mistakes as he wandered aimlessly, still unsure of his way around the vast building? Did they know that he had wheeled a ninety-year-old woman into the maternity ward and that Nader had slapped his thighs and laughed with his bright white Arab teeth when he heard about it? Did Axel know that he was losing his grip? That he sat on the sofa with the kitten all day long, seeking refuge in substance abuse, that he was no longer capable of taking pleasure in anything but turned to the Koran, actively seeking condemnation in order to torment himself and to atone for what they had done? Perhaps the trip to Dead

Water is a trap? He shuddered. Axel wants to make sure he's still in control. He will never give that up. I've got to be on my guard.

His mother looked perplexed as she opened the door.

'Philip,' she said. 'Is that you? Is something wrong?'

Instantly she thought that something bad had happened. It was as if she could smell it. She looked at him through greasy spectacles before quickly raising her hand and patting him on the arm. As always, her hair was aggressively permed, and she wore down-at-heel sandals that creaked as she walked. He entered and passed her. There was a smell of fried food mixed with sour tobacco coming from the kitchen.

'No,' he said, not looking at her. 'I'm just here to get something.'

She closed the door after him and walked through the house. The floorboards creaked too. She sounded like an old cart rolling across the floor. She was very bowlegged. It had got worse over the years, as if her bones were softening. You could roll a barrel through those legs, he thought.

'But you can stay for a while, can't you?' she asked. 'I've got fresh spice cake. Sit down and I'll make you a cup of coffee. By the way, have you seen the newspapers? They found that boy, you know the one who went missing right before Christmas. You were at that party with him. Did you see it, Philip? About the Vietnamese boy.'

'Yes.'

She disappeared into the kitchen and called towards the living room.

'Have the police been round to talk to you again?'

'Yes,' he said. 'They're talking to everyone. It's the same drill as before. They've interviewed all sixteen of us again.'

He sat down in an armchair and drummed his fingers on the armrest while he listened to the sounds coming from the kitchen, the clattering of cups, running water, a knife on a chopping board. Everything about her was energetic and there was force behind everything she did, a raw decisive power. Five minutes later she returned with a tray. He thought that some of her greying hair was bordering on green, like lichen in the mountains. He wanted to give her something, but he was far too wound up to be generous, so he replied mechanically to all her questions.

'And what about Axel?' she wanted to know.

'Well, Axel,' he said evasively. 'We stick together, you know. As always.'

'It must be strange Jon not being there,' she said.

'Yes,' he said. 'It is strange.'

'Poor Jon Moreno.'

'Yes, that was bad.'

'I've heard some nasty rumours,' she said.

His heart skipped a beat.

'That you couldn't carry his coffin. That you dropped it with a crash.'

'Some dog ruined it all,' he said. 'It came at us and we lost our balance.'

'Oh? They said it was a white poodle.'

He helped himself to a slice of spice cake. It crumbled into small pieces, which he pushed together with his fingers. She sat down across from him. Her faded dress was covered with tiny holes from cigarette sparks.

'So what have you come to get?' she asked, munching her cake. 'The shed is nearly empty, you know, there's nothing there, Philip, no clothes or old sports equipment. You and sports, ha ha. I can picture it. You in hockey clothes, Philip. Or swinging a golf club.'

Reilly slurped his coffee. He watched her furtively. She might be unkempt, but she was no fool. Her mouth lived a life of its own. All sorts of superficial nonsense poured out of her mouth, while her brain reasoned sharply and wisely. But she was not sentimental. She dealt only in reality. She had made her fair share of packed lunches for him over the years, she had put her clumsy signature on his school report, she had washed his clothes, she had cooked and cleaned and put food on the table. And she thought that this made her a mother. I don't like you, he thought, but you would never notice because it requires a sensitivity which you don't possess.

'No,' he cleared his throat. 'This is something I've always wanted. And it's not as if you need it.'

She frowned.

'Dad's old revolver.'

She put down her cup with a bang. He thought the saucer would shatter.

'Revolver? What do you want that for?'

He managed a smile though it felt like a snarl.

'I've always fancied that revolver,' he said. 'It's my inheritance. The fact that it was in the war appeals to me.'

She wiped her mouth with the back of her hand. Her fingers were stained yellow with nicotine.

'But, strictly speaking, you're not legally allowed to have it, are you?' she said. 'Dad had a licence. You don't. Or have you got yourself a licence?'

He tried to act casual. 'It's not as if I'm thinking of shooting anyone,' he said. 'I just want to have it lying around. In a drawer.'

She took a second piece of cake and started to chew with her mouth open. Her tongue was pale and grey.

'Of course you can have the old revolver,' she said. 'I'm just surprised, that's all. You've never mentioned it before, and it's been here for God knows how many years. And you're a man of peace, so to speak. But you need to keep it in a locked cabinet. You could get fined.'

'I will. Don't nag.'

He took another slice of cake from the plate. There was nothing wrong with her baking. The cake tasted of cinnamon, ginger and cardamom and it was rich with butter. His fingers were greasy.

'I've got myself a kitten,' he said.

'God Almighty. What are you going to do with it?'

She reached for the pouch of Petterøe loose tobacco lying on the coffee table and fished out a pinch.

'A kitten?' she said again. 'Please tell me it's not a female, it'll

143

have kittens before you know it. They'll take over your whole flat and then you're stuck with them. You'll end up having to drown them in a tub because nobody wants them. They're nothing but trouble.'

'It's a tom,' he said quickly. 'It keeps me company. But it's an indoor cat. It follows me everywhere. It lies in my lap and on my bed.'

'You'll never grow up,' she declared. 'A kitten in your bed. You're a grown man. Anyone would think you'd been deprived of something when you were little.'

Her lips tightened around the cigarette. Sparks scattered in her lap, but she was oblivious to them.

They sat at the coffee table for a while. She chatted away. He was happy to make the right noises, and she did not register his lack of interest. Then he thanked her for the coffee and cake, pushed back his chair and nodded towards the cabinet where his father's old Enfield revolver was kept. Next to the weapon was a box of ammunition. He took that from the cabinet as well.

'You're taking the bullets too?' she frowned. 'What do you need them for?'

'They're part of it,' he said. 'Aren't you pleased to be rid of them?'

'They must be stored separately,' she dictated. 'The bullets. And the revolver. It's the law.'

It seemed as though she had changed her mind and wanted to hold on to the revolver after all. A sudden suspicion had flared up in her eyes.

'But you've been storing them in the same cabinet all the time,' he protested.

She shrugged. Then she hurried out into the kitchen and started opening cupboards.

'There's something else,' she called out, 'as you're here with your hand out anyway.'

He waited patiently. He held the revolver with awe; it was surprisingly heavy. He heard clattering and mumbling. Now where did I leave it, and then, oh yes, there it is. My, oh my, it's good stuff this. Finally he heard a brief laugh. She reappeared. He stared at the object in her hands. A glass bottle in the shape of a Viking ship.

'Cognac,' she explained. 'Dad got it for his fiftieth birthday, remember? From his mates at the foundry.'

'Cognac?' he said.

'Yes, do you get it? Your ship has come in,' she giggled. 'I believe it's very good cognac too, but alcohol in a ship-shaped bottle is ridiculous. Take it, please,' she ordered him. 'It's Larsen. I don't drink cognac.'

'Neither do I,' he said.

'And it's well matured now,' she went on, as though she hadn't heard him. 'Remember, it needs to be served at room temperature.'

He accepted the cognac ship. He felt like an idiot.

'I don't drink cognac,' he repeated.

She continued to ignore him.

'You never know what life might throw at you,' she went on, 'and the day will come when you'll need a stiff cognac, believe you me. Then you'll be glad you have some Larsen. Real men drink cognac,' she concluded.

He nodded. He moved towards the door in an attempt to leave. She followed him in her creaking sandals.

'I was wondering,' she said. 'Do you still see Valentino?'

She meant Axel.

'Is he one of those who prefer men?' she wanted to know. She winked at him as she said it.

Reilly shrugged. 'That's just a joke. He flirts with everyone.'

'He certainly is a bit peculiar,' she said, shaking her head. Her curls didn't move a millimetre. But she was smiling now. Women tended to do that whenever they thought of Axel Frimann.

'I need something to carry this in,' Reilly said.

She popped into a closet and came out holding a dreadful plastic bag with pink handles.

'That's the worst bag I've ever seen,' he said. 'I can't walk down the street with that.'

'Have you turned into a show-off like Axel?' she asked.

That evening he got very high. Afterwards he went on the Internet to read about the revolver he now owned. There were several models, but he soon pinpointed the one lying on the table. It had been in his family since the war and was a British handgun produced by the government-owned Royal Small Arms Factory in Enfield. The first model was used by the police and a later one had been standard issue in the Second World War. The revolver weighed 765 grams and the chamber held six bullets. He also learned that when he cocked the hammer he could fire all six bullets in one sequence. He got up from his chair, raised the revolver and aimed it at a jar on the windowsill. Axel may have made plans, he thought. But with this in my hand, I'm in control.

CHAPTER 30

Sejer was kneeling by his wife's grave, shivering in the cold. His dog, Frank Robert, waited patiently while he dug at random in the soil of the small bed where nothing grew. Please forgive me, Elise, he was thinking, I could have brought a rose. But the years pass. I've stopped looking over my shoulder. I know now that you won't be there. Yoo Van Chau is still sitting in her chair listening out for footsteps. In brief moments she forgets what has happened. It takes a long time before it sinks in.

He got up and stuck his hands in his pockets.

But I won all the same, he thought. I won the biggest prize life's lottery had to offer. I found you, and I got to have you with me for many years.

Elise. My first prize.

He left the cemetery and, still shivering, headed for the riverside promenade. It started to rain. The river was more turbulent than usual. It tumbled by with unstoppable force and whipped up white foam around the bridge supports. He followed the whirling currents with his eyes; they looked like boiling black cauldrons in the water. The rain got heavier. The dog looked up at him. Isn't it time we got going? it seemed to be thinking. It's freezing cold.

The worst thing about losing someone, Sejer thought, is the fear of further loss. One brick falls out and the whole wall is at risk. After the death of Elise he had grown terrified of losing his daughter. He imagined that his wife's death had pointed a spotlight on his family, and in its revealing glare the devil himself could see them and would strike again.

'We are going to stand here for a while and be cold,' he told the dog.

'We owe that to Elise.'

That night he had a dream. It was evening, and he was waiting at a bus stop with Frank Robert. After a long wait the bus arrived with lit-up windows and they both went inside where it was warm. Sejer rummaged around in his pockets for loose change and temporarily had to let go of the leash. Before he had time to turn around, Frank had jumped off the bus. He was just about to run after him when the accordion-style door closed and the bus drove off. Sejer asked the bus driver to stop.

'You'll have to wait. I've got a timetable to stick to.'

'How far is the next stop?' Sejer asked.

'Far,' the bus driver said. 'Sit down.'

He found a seat by the window. He was unsettled because he had lost Frank. He stared out of the window. It was dark outside and there was not much to look at. He did not know where he was, either, it was an unknown landscape, and he could not see how Frank would be able to find his own way back to the flat. His imagination worked overtime. The dog might get run over by a truck and would have to be carried off in a sack.

He continued to stare out of the window. No one was out in the cold and there were long stretches with no lights. When the bus finally stopped, he jumped off and started running back. He kept calling Frank Robert's name. He zigzagged across paths and tracks and through small groves, but the small grey Shar Pei seemed to have vanished into thin air.

A girl appeared in the dark.

'There's a kennel up that road,' she said. 'They take all the strays there.'

She pointed as she told him this. Sejer started running again. He reached a building that looked like a barn, found the entrance, flung open the door and explained why he had come. A man took him to a large room. Sejer looked inside and his heart sank because he knew he would never be able to find Frank among this multitude of dogs. They were all Shar Peis and they were all grey.

He awoke with a start. He lay awake for a long time. How can I apply that, he wondered, what I have learned, my knowledge of grief and death? How much can words help? I could discover an explanation and give it to Yoo Van Chau, but that would not be enough. She wants it to make sense. What would she say if I were to tell her she had won first prize in life's lottery? He switched on his lamp and looked down at the floor. Frank Robert was sleeping with his head on his paws.

CHAPTER 31

Axel turned up that Friday at six o'clock in a silver Nissan Micra.

'What is that?' Reilly said. He gawped at the small vehicle.

Axel patted the roof of the car. 'It's a rental car,' he said. 'The police have picked up my Mercedes and taken it to forensics.'

'Why?'

'It needs to be examined as part of their investigation,' Axel explained. 'We've got to make do with this.'

Reilly looked at the car dubiously. He was holding a bag. Inside it was a warm sweater. Wrapped in the sweater were the Koran and the Enfield revolver with six bullets in its chambers. At his feet stood a small travel kennel. The kitten peered nervously out through the bars.

'Are you sure that's a real car?' Reilly said. 'And not a Christmas decoration?'

'Have you got the letter?' Axel asked. 'Give it to me. I want to have a look at the bloody thing.'

Reilly pulled the envelope from his back pocket.

Axel tore out the sheet and held it up to the light.

'No self-respecting man would use this kind of stationery,' he said. 'This is a woman's writing paper.'

He folded the sheet, put it in his pocket and opened the boot. Reilly placed his bag next to Axel's backpack and a cardboard box of groceries.

He left the kennel with the kitten on the back seat.

After a few kilometres the kitten started to drool.

'He's travel-sick,' Reilly explained.

'Is he going to throw up?' Axel frowned.

'If he does, he'll only throw up inside the cage,' Reilly said, 'and I've lined it with newspaper.'

Axel braked and turned into a Shell petrol station. 'I forgot something,' he said. 'Won't be a minute.'

He disappeared into the shop and returned with a carrier bag. Reilly heard him open the boot and rummage around. Then he was back behind the wheel.

'I've bought some great food,' he said. 'Free-range pork.'

'What kind of pork is that?' Reilly asked.

'From pigs that have been reared out in the open. They've never been confined in crates with other pigs.'

Reilly wondered if Axel might be having a laugh at his expense.

'You want me to believe it tastes better than any other pork?'

'Of course. A free pig is a happy pig, and a happy pig is a tasty pig.'

'Now I get it,' Reilly said. 'A happy pig is a more expensive pig. And we can't tell the difference anyway.'

'I can,' Axel said. 'Pigs in crates can't even turn around. They spend their whole lives standing up, crammed together, biting each other.'

'I can't imagine who might have sent that letter,' Reilly said.

It was nearly nine in the evening when they pulled up at the grass bank in front of the cabin. They made two trips with the luggage, which they dumped on the floor, and then they lit the paraffin lamps. Reilly disappeared into his usual bedroom. He placed his bag next to his bed and made a disturbing discovery. The zip was not completely closed. Hadn't he shut it properly? He unzipped the bag and looked inside. At the top lay a carrier bag from Shell containing paprika-flavoured crisps.

'Did you open my bag?' he called out.

Axel called back. 'Is that a problem? My backpack was full.'

Reilly rummaged around in his bag. He made sure that the revolver was still there, inside the sweater. This new situation unsettled him. Perhaps he had already lost control? He shoved the bag under his bed, stood up and chewed his thumbnail.

'Are you coming?' Axel shouted. 'We need to start cooking the pork.' He looked in to see Reilly standing by the bed.

'What's up? You look weird.'

Reilly let the kitten out of the cage. It padded around and explored every corner of the room. Axel went out into the kitchen. He opened the package of pork fillet and held the large, pink lump of meat in his hands.

'Here's the free-range piggy,' he said, 'and look how happy he is.'

He took a knife from a drawer and placed it on a chopping board. It was a heavy-duty knife with a rubber handle, a long slim blade and a blood groove. A knife like that handles well. Reilly shuddered. It has superb grip. That knife can cut straight to the bone. He started to sweat. He was not sure he was in control. His body yearned for the feeling of well-being that the drugs normally induced. Perhaps he ought to get high?

'Peel the potatoes,' Axel ordered him. He shoved a bag in Reilly's direction.

Reilly kept an eye on the kitten, which was still wandering around the cabin.

'We need to keep the doors closed,' he remembered. 'If the kitten gets out, he won't be able to find his way back.'

'But he was born here,' Axel reminded him. 'And he needs to pee and much more besides. Go and find an old crate in the shed and make some sort of litter box for him. Get some sand from the shore.'

He cut the meat into suitably sized steaks, lit the gas stove and melted butter in the frying pan. He set the table and opened a bottle of red wine.

Later, over dinner, Axel looked at him for a long time.

'How long have we known each other?' he asked.

Reilly did the mental arithmetic.

'We first met when we were six years old and now we're twenty-five. That's nineteen years.'

He stuck his fork into the free-range pork.

'Friendships like that don't grow on trees,' Axel said. 'Nineteen years. That's a lifetime.'

Reilly nodded.

'It takes a long time to build a friendship,' Axel went on. 'Think about all the people you meet during your life. At different stages. At nursery and at school, when you're travelling or studying, at work. At parties, in the street and in shops. How many of them become friends for life?'

Reilly waited for Axel to continue.

'Hardly any of them,' Axel said. 'Friendship is worth much more than love. Friendship is a commitment. Don't you agree?'

'Yes,' Reilly said.

'I think Jon reneged on his obligations,' Axel said.

'We'll never know,' Reilly said.

'The letter,' Axel said.

'The business with the letter is totally bizarre,' Reilly said, 'but we can't blame Jon because we can't be certain.'

They looked at each other across the table.

'It's noble of you to think well of Jon, but being naive is dangerous.' Suddenly he smiled a warm and broad smile. 'A toast to humanity,' he said, raising his glass. 'A toast to God and His mysterious ways. And a toast to women who spread their legs for us. At least if we ask them nicely.'

After dinner they walked down to Dead Water.

From the shore they studied the surface of the lake, and they were mesmerised by its black sheen for a long time.

'Dare we go out there?' Axel said.

'In the boat, you mean?'

'No, on foot.'

Reilly snorted.

'Everyone can walk on water,' Axel claimed. 'It's merely a matter of weight distribution.'

Reilly picked a rush and started chewing it. He moved a couple of steps to the side. He did not like Axel being too close; you never knew what was on his mind. But Axel copied his movements.

'Don't let them get you,' he said. 'Don't let them put you in a cell. It'll kill you.'

Reilly stared at the point where Jon had let himself fall into the water. 'I'm going to die sooner or later,' he said. 'It's just a matter of time. I thought we agreed on that.'

'Listen to me,' Axel said. 'This is serious. You will go mad. You won't be able to take drugs either, not regularly, anyway. You'll be sitting on your bunk, your teeth chattering, and no one will care about you. The prison service doesn't waste resources on someone like you. They can't be bothered to rehabilitate a scabby old drug addict. No one will visit you either. Who would come, Reilly? Do you think Nader will turn up and read aloud to you from the Koran?'

Reilly started walking back towards the cabin. He wanted to be with the kitten. He needed to get high. He wanted to curl up in a chair in front of the fire. Axel's words were starting to get to him.

'Putting someone in a prison cell is a form of assault,' Axel said.

Reilly carried on walking.

'And no one will want you when you get out, either,' Axel shouted after him. 'No one will give you a job or a place to live. Do you think that's what you deserve?'

Reilly ran the last bit of the way and tore open the door.

'That's exactly what I deserve,' he said. 'And so do you.'

The fire had died down. Only a few red embers remained.

Axel rose from his chair and started clearing up. He was signalling that the evening had come to an end, like someone shutting a café.

Time, gentlemen.

Time for bed.

Reilly stood up. He was a little unsteady. The high which had lifted him for the last hour was leaving his body. It slithered away like a snake and took its sweet poison. He carried bottles and glasses out into the kitchen. He quickly checked the cutlery drawer to see if the carving knife with the rubber handle was back in its place. It was missing.

Axel entered with two sleeping bags.

'Blue or green?' he wanted to know.

'Blue,' Reilly replied.

The sleeping bag was rolled up tightly inside a nylon bag. Reilly went to his bedroom and tossed it on the bed, where it bounced and rolled back and forth on the foam mattress.

Axel leaned lazily against the doorframe.

'Do you remember what we used to call Jon when we were kids?' Reilly asked.

Axel did. 'We called him Toten Transport. That was what it said on his dad's truck. It was the name of the company he worked for. Jon had a cap with their logo. Sometimes we just called him Toten. Why do you ask about that now?'

'Don't know,' Reilly mumbled.

'You think too much,' Axel said.

Reilly fetched the kitten.

'I'll make breakfast tomorrow,' Axel said. 'Is that kitten going in the sleeping bag with you?'

'Yes.'

'Before I go to bed there's something important that I want to say to you,' Axel said. 'I understand people.'

'Right.'

'I see straight through them and I know their motives. And their intentions. I'm always one step ahead. If you get my drift.'

'Stop bothering me.'

'Pleasant dreams,' Axel said.

Reilly closed the door. Axel washed up after dinner, he thought, and I dried. I don't recall drying the carving knife. What the hell has he done with it? He dug the revolver out of the bag and crept inside his sleeping bag, still fully dressed. Now that the door was closed he was surrounded by dense, cool darkness. The kitten curled up against the wall. Reilly lay very still with the revolver in his hand. He focused all his energy on listening, and the sounds amplified: something was being pushed or pulled across the living room floor. Sharp cracks he could not identify. And there was the sound of heavy breathing, but perhaps that was coming from him. Mustn't fall asleep, he told himself, mustn't doze off; suddenly he'll be looming over me with the knife and it'll go right in between my ribs. Afterwards he'll throw me in Dead Water and I'll end up under the mud like a rotting log. Then the secret will be safe. That's what he wants. That's why he dragged me up here. I've known it all the time, but I'm ready for him.

He placed his hand on the kitten. Its vertebrae felt like tiny bumps under its fur. No one knows I'm here, he remembered. No one would know where to look. He was sure he could hear footsteps in the living room. He was also convinced he could hear noises coming from the room that lay furthest away and which used to be Jon's. As if Jon had been sleeping in there all along and was now waking up, and the whole thing had been a nightmare. Of course he hadn't drowned himself. It all seemed incomprehensible to Reilly. Jon sank to the bottom, he thought, and we just watched. We rowed away. We went to bed. We lied to Ingerid. We're second-class citizens.

Suddenly his door opened. Light from the living room poured in. Axel was standing in the doorway. Reilly clutched the revolver inside his sleeping bag.

'I was just wondering,' Axel said. 'If someone were to give you a million. Would you bite the head off a viper?'

'A live viper?'

'Very much alive.'

'Of course not. Why do you ask? Have you completely lost the plot?'

'Just wanted to know if you had balls. You don't,' he declared.

Then he left. Floorboards creaked as he walked away. Reilly noticed that Axel hadn't shut the door completely so he carefully shifted the kitten and wriggled out of the sleeping bag to close it. Axel had planted an image in his head, and it was unbearable. He had a taste of rot in his mouth and a feeling of nausea in his throat and stomach, as though a headless snake was squirming down there. He crept back inside the sleeping bag. He deliberately did not zip it up but lay there alert, waiting. It was getting stormy outside, the wind went through the wooden cabin with a violent, compelling force. The door opened a second time. Axel entered.

'I forgot something,' he said. 'That bloody tooth of mine has started to hurt again. You don't happen to have some paracetamol?'

Reilly hoisted himself up on one elbow.

'No,' he said.

'Or some Pinex? Ibuprofen? Paralgin?'

Reilly shook his head. He did not understand where Axel was going with this. He's summoning up his courage, he thought. The third time he'll strike. He'll wait until dawn, and then he'll come. But I can wait, I can stay awake, and I have six bullets in the chambers.

When Axel had left for the second time, Reilly leaned over the edge of the bed and retrieved his bag. He took out the Koran, which was at the bottom, found a box of matches in the drawer of the bedside table and lit the paraffin lamp. He began to read. After a while he started to calm down. The text settled him. His life acquired a sense of direction. The kitten lay snuggled against the wall, purring. The wind took hold, nature surrendered and the door was opened for the third time. Reilly dropped the Koran and fumbled for the revolver.

'What about the tip of your little finger,' Axel asked. 'Would you sacrifice the tip of your little finger for a million?'

Reilly groaned. 'You've got to stop bothering me.'

'You still don't have the balls,' Axel said. 'And you're not greedy either. How are you going to manage?'

'Are you worried about me?' Reilly asked.

Axel was now halfway across the threshold. Reilly could not

see his right hand. Perhaps he was holding the knife. Any moment now he might leap across the room. It would only take him a few seconds.

'Don't stay up reading for too long,' Axel said gruffly. 'The light is bad. You'll damage your eyes. My mum told me so.'

'What else did your mum tell you?' Reilly asked.

'To always think the worst of people. Here you are, my best friend, reading the Koran. With your kitten asleep by your side. An image like that is just too good to be true. What do you say, Reilly? Is it true?'

'Go to bed,' Reilly growled.

'Why do you still have all your clothes on when you're in your sleeping bag?' Axel wanted to know.

'Because it's chilly in here.'

'Don't forget your evening prayers. Allah is great, or whatever you say?'

'Are you scared of the dark?' Reilly asked. 'Since you keep running back to my room?'

Axel made no reply. Instead he calmly retired. Reilly heard his footsteps crossing the floor. He heard a door slamming. And a murmur from the woods rose out of the silence at Dead Water.

CHAPTER 32

Sejer suggested to Frank Robert that the two of them might like to share a beer. Frank Robert immediately ran to the kitchen and sat in front of the fridge. Sejer opened a can and poured half its contents into the dog's bowl before sitting in his chair by the window. He heard the dog slurp beer in the kitchen and remembered that it was rather overweight, especially around its stomach. However, he was unsure whether this was due to the beer or to all the leftovers it got. His train of thought was interrupted by the doorbell ringing. Jacob Skarre was standing outside. He was neither flushed nor out of breath.

'You took the lift,' Sejer remarked.

'You live on the thirteenth floor,' Skarre protested.

He shrugged.

'It's late, I know,' he said. 'Tell me if it's a bad time, and I'll be off at once. I just happened to be in your neck of the woods.'

Sejer beckoned him inside. 'Don't go,' he said. 'It's fine. Come in. We can have a whisky, and you can leave your car here.'

They each settled down with a glass. Skarre took in the view of the gleaming river deep below. A goods train slowly glided into the station. From the thirteenth floor it looked like a Märklin toy train.

'You've got a wonderful view,' he commented.

'Yes,' Sejer said. 'Every evening I sit here and look down on people.'

'You've never looked down on anyone,' Skarre said.

He tasted his whisky. It was room temperature.

'I went to see Ingerid Moreno today,' Skarre said. 'She told me about Jon. About what his life had been like. He was born two months premature. When they examined him, they discovered he had only one kidney. When he was five, he developed allergies to grass pollen and a range of foods. When he was nine, he went straight over the handlebars of his bicycle and sustained minor brain damage which resulted in epilepsy. He grew out of that eventually, but he was on medication for years. When he was thirteen, he got cerebrospinal meningitis and very nearly died. And when he was sixteen, he suffered acute appendicitis which led to peritonitis. He underwent surgery at the last minute. Nature was clearly determined to torment him from the start.'

'What about Frimann?' Sejer asked. 'What did you discover about him?'

'He has distinguished himself his whole life,' Skarre said. 'First at school and later in the army. Clever. Popular. Ambitious. When it comes to Philip Reilly, the picture becomes more blurred. Not a shining light at school. Rather introverted and passive. A series of casual jobs which he performs adequately, but not terribly well. He gets high a lot. His current job as a hospital porter is in jeopardy after several incidents of carelessness. And there is something else I've noticed, a little oddity, which might have no significance whatsoever. Reilly, Van Chau and Moreno are all only children, and they all grew up completely or partially without a father.'

'What about the relationship between them?' Sejer said. 'How would you describe that?'

'Jon never asserted himself much, but perhaps he preferred being part of a group,' Skarre said. 'And this need led him to Axel and Reilly. Reilly is characterised by this strange passivity which prevents him from ever taking a stand, while Axel assumes the lead in every situation. And because he is strong and charismatic, the others followed him. Anywhere, possibly. But we've no chance of getting them convicted. We don't even know what happened and we don't have enough evidence to charge them. The only thing that could help us would be a confession.'

He drank his room-temperature whisky.

'And we can forget about that.'

Afterwards they took the dog for a walk.

They crossed the car park in front of Sejer's block of flats and turned on to a path. Frank Robert was let off his leash. He had a flashing blue light attached to his collar so he was clearly visible even when he darted in between the trees. Skarre's eyes followed the blue light.

'Dogs can sniff out drugs,' Skarre said, 'and explosives. And corpses. Some dogs can detect rot in timber. Scientists believe they might even be able to sniff out cancer. Imagine if we could teach them to detect guilt. Then we could take a dog to Frimann and Reilly and it would smell their guilt straight away.' He stopped to light a cigarette. 'But we can't be sure that they meant to commit a crime. Incidentally, some people claim that criminality can be measured,' he said.

'And how is that done?' Sejer asked.

'An American professor has designed a scale from one to twenty-two. He gives the example of a woman who shot and killed her husband because he was having an affair. She caught him with someone else and acted on impulse. She scored only two points on the scale.'

'We don't own each other,' Sejer remarked. 'She got off lightly.'

'And then there's Ted Bundy,' Skarre continued. 'He scores seventeen points.'

'Who scores twenty-two?' Sejer asked.

'Many top the scale,' Skarre said. 'John Edward Robinson, Dennis Rader. Kemper, Holmes and Sells. And John Wayne Gacy. And I am getting to the point. I'm making a point, I promise. Just because you're to blame for something, doesn't mean that you accept that blame. Or that you feel guilty. Gacy killed more than thirty people, but he said it was like squashing cockroaches. When he was finally caught, he went on about his childhood and how awful it had been. He spoke the following classic line when he was put in prison: "I'm the real victim here."'

Skarre took a puff of his cigarette. 'If we're lucky we might nail Axel Frimann. And I have a strong feeling he'll say the same thing.'

The telephone was ringing when they unlocked the front door and entered the hall.

Forensics had completed their examination of Axel Frimann's Mercedes.

'A fair amount of time has passed and the car was cleaned very thoroughly, probably on several occasions. No evidence from Kim Van Chau was found in the front or the back seats or on the floor. No fingerprints or other biological trace.'

Sejer received the information with great composure. 'I wouldn't expect them to carry a dead body inside the car,' he said. 'Get to the point. What about the rest of it?'

'Precisely. In the boot we did discover some evidence, and we are certain that it belongs to Kim Van Chau.'

'Evidence. What kind of evidence?'

'The boot was lined with a blanket. And Frimann has undoubtedly hoovered it, but Asian hair is very coarse. It locks into the fibres.'

'Are you sure of your evidence? Is it a full match?'

'Absolutely. And this means that Kim's body was definitely transported in Frimann's car.'

CHAPTER 33

Reilly awoke with a shudder.

There was someone in his room. Someone was standing in a corner, breathing softly. He sensed movement, detected a faint smell. He fumbled around the sleeping bag for the revolver. The darkness was so compact that it was impossible to see anything. Even the kitten was startled. It clambered over him and jumped on to the floor. He became aware of an even denser darkness which might be the outline of a man by the door. The black mass was immobile, poised as if it were watching him. Reilly propped himself up on one elbow.

'Axel?' he whispered.

No reply. All he heard was the wind. It had dropped considerably, and the morning was not far off. He eased himself into a sitting position, keeping the weapon ready all the time. His heart was pounding and it was difficult to keep the revolver still. Was that a glimmer of light in the darkness, the blade of a knife, or the gleam in Axel's eye? He could not be sure. He wriggled out of the sleeping bag and stood up. He could no longer make out the black mass by the door. He tiptoed across the floor. Every nerve on edge. There was no one there. His hands felt only timber with the occasional splinter in the walls. He opened the door as noiselessly as he could and peeked into the living room. A barely perceptible grey light fell through the windows, and the back of a chair was just visible. Reilly still thought he heard breathing. He crept across the room and stopped at Axel's door. It was a simple pine door with a plastic handle. He clutched the butt of the revolver and eased the door open. Grey light from the living room seeped in. The green sleeping bag on the bed reminded him

163

of a limp cucumber. He had no idea how long he stood like that, his arms dangling, the mouth of the gun pointing towards the floor.

Axel came at him from behind. Reilly was yanked backwards and crashed to the floor. The revolver slipped out of his hand, skidded across the floor and hit the wall with a bang.

'Are you trying to shoot me?' Axel cried. 'Eh?'

He put his arm around Reilly's neck and squeezed as hard as he could. Axel was strong. Reilly could hardly breathe. All he could do was kick his legs, but that did not help him get air into his lungs.

'I'm always one step ahead!' Axel screamed. 'Don't you understand?'

The grip around his neck tightened. Reilly tried to force out a reply; he could only manage some unintelligible grunts, and while he lay there, growing weaker because of oxygen deprivation, it dawned on him that he wanted to give up, that it no longer mattered to him either way. Jon couldn't cope with being alive and neither can I, Reilly thought. He was starting to black out. His head felt very hot.

'I understand people and I see through them,' Axel snarled. Reilly felt his breath in his ear. The smell of Axel, his raw strength.

'You can't even put up a proper fight,' Axel said. 'You don't deserve to live.'

Reilly wanted to beg for mercy. He wanted to explain and to put forward a proposal, but he couldn't get a word out. Finally Axel let go of him. Reilly filled his lungs with air, but he was too terrified to move. Something in his throat had been badly hurt and he did not know if he still had a voice.

Axel got up and stared at Reilly lying on the floor.

'So what the hell were you doing?'

'I was unsettled,' Reilly said. 'I heard something.' He tried to work out what he was feeling. He realised he did not feel much of anything. Now I know why people kill, he thought. They're scared.

'Would you have shot me?' Axel asked. 'You would have, wouldn't you?'

He picked up the revolver. He opened the chamber and looked inside.

'Six bullets. Bloody hell.'

Reilly dragged himself to standing. He massaged his neck for a while, then staggered to a chair and collapsed. After some time he began to recover; he got up and fetched the kitten. He put it inside the travel kennel. He gathered his belongings and packed them in his bag, along with his toiletries, his spare sweater and the Koran. Finally he put on his long coat.

Reilly did everything at a very slow pace.

Axel watched him calmly. 'And where do you think you're going?' he asked.

'Home,' Reilly replied. 'I'm going home to my flat.'

'Walking, are you? You intend to plod along the road with that cage in your hand? Do you know what time it is?'

Reilly opened the front door and went outside on to the grass bank.

'You look like a ghost in that coat,' Axel shouted after him. 'No one's going to give you a lift.'

Reilly left. His coat-tails flapped, the travel kennel swung in his hand. After an hour trudging along the narrow track through the woods, he reached the main road, and later that morning a lorry driver transporting timber gave him a lift.

CHAPTER 34

He fed the kitten.

He watched it eat.

I've dithered my whole life, he thought, but now I'm going to be a man of action.

When the kitten had finished its food, it curled up in a corner and went to sleep. Reilly looked around the flat. He had made a decision and he was determined. His eyes fell on the Viking ship bottle his mother had given him. It sat on a shelf above the window. Carefully he took it down, held it up to the light and admired the colour of the liquid. The day has come when I need a stiff cognac, he said to himself.

He took a clean glass from a cupboard and poured himself a drink. This will do the job, he thought. Next he needed a notepad and a pen, which he found in the kitchen. He pottered around for a while. He had several things to take care of. He still felt a strong determination calmly propelling him on.

The kitten was sleeping. Reilly opened the kitchen window to get some fresh air. He looked down on the black tarmac. It was wet after a brief shower, but the sun shone now. Reilly sat down to write his confession. He forced himself to think back, to try to comprehend how the party at Skjæret had led him to this point. Again he looked out of the window. He spotted a seagull soaring on a current of air. The sight of the white bird moved him. He got the idea that someone had sent it as a sign. The bird was proof of a purpose, which had finally made itself known elegantly.

He looked at the kitten.

John Coffey had a mouse, he thought, it had lived in his cell and he had called it Mr Jingles. Perry Smith had a squirrel. And

I have a kitten. What will become of you? Perhaps you'll be put down and then ground into pet food. Perhaps a Rottweiler will eat you for breakfast, literally. For a long time such thoughts tormented him. Then he started to write. The pen moved swiftly, the words came easily. He forgot time and place because he was back in the flat with Irene. Philip Reilly wrote. The sun rose in the sky, sending a beam through the window. It warmed his neck. He lived on a quiet street and today was a Saturday, but every now and then a car would drive past. At times he could hear people's voices. And then there was the sound of a car door slamming. The car seemed to have stopped outside his block, but no one was likely to visit him at this time in the morning. He wasn't expecting anyone so he carried on writing. When the doorbell rang, he sat chewing his pen for a while. The interruption weakened his resolve. But someone did see us, he thought. I have been expecting this moment.

He went to open the door. Axel burst in.

'God's peace, Reilly. That's how you Muslims greet each other, isn't it?'

Axel was holding the revolver. He went inside and sat down at the kitchen table where he instantly noticed the Viking ship filled with cognac.

'Good God, what have you got here? I didn't know you had such a naff side to you,' he said. 'Cognac in a ship?'

He twisted and turned the ship, and after studying it thoroughly, he put it down again.

'Do you remember when we were kids?' he asked. 'Do you remember what we did on rainy days?'

Reilly was unable to answer. Axel had disrupted his momentum and he lost his train of thought.

'We would go outside and squash snails,' Axel said. 'When it rained they would crawl out of the ditch and on to the tarmac. Once we saw more than a hundred just on the way to the corner shop.'

Reilly knew what was coming next.

'And we would step on them,' Axel said. 'A trail of slime followed us all the way to the sweetshop.'

'Why are you going on about the snails now?' Reilly asked.

'Because you distinguished yourself even then,' Axel said. 'You were so calculating. If you put your foot on the snail's head, a kind of green slime would come out. But if you placed your foot on its tail, some disgusting yellow substance that looked like butter would squirt out. It was a choice you made every time you lifted your foot. Green or yellow.'

'They were just snails,' Reilly protested.

Axel noticed the notepad on the table.

'What are you writing?' he asked. 'I hope you're not snitching?'

He grabbed the notepad.

'It's just some nonsense I'm writing for myself,' Reilly mumbled.

Axel read a few lines and then slammed his fist on the table.

'Could we help it?' he barked. 'Did we intend to hurt Kim?'

'No,' Reilly stuttered.

Axel lost his composure. Reilly had never seen him so irate. His anger has been latent the whole time, he thought, and now it's come to the surface.

'Do you know what evil is?' Axel yelled. 'What is evil, Reilly? Do you want me to show you?'

Reilly had no time to react. Axel strode to the corner and grabbed the kitten. He held it in his hands, in his fists of steel. The kitten started to squeal. A high-pitched, heart-breaking wail that broke Reilly's heart. Axel moved to the open kitchen window. He held the kitten by the neck, leaned out and looked down at the tarmac.

'This is evil,' he said.

And he hurled the kitten out of the window.

It flew through the air like a small grey and white ball.

Reilly staggered to his bed and collapsed. The sight of the kitten being thrown from the window was more than he could take. He struggled to breathe. He clenched his fists so hard that his nails dug into his palms. The kitten falling out of the window, he thought, like a tiny flying squirrel with splayed legs. The kitten hitting the tarmac head first. He wanted to beat Axel to a pulp. He tensed every muscle as he sat there on the edge of the bed, gathering the necessary strength.

Axel was sitting down at the kitchen table again. He raised the glass of cognac and held it up to the light. What happened next was such a shock that Reilly forgot all about attacking Axel. He simply stared at him, barely able to believe his own eyes. It would appear that the kitten killer needed some Dutch courage. He lifted the glass to his lips and drained it in one gulp.

Reilly had watched closely and he was not mistaken. The glass was empty and the cognac was now inside Axel, where its considerable effect would soon manifest itself.

'What did you put in the cognac?' Axel frowned. 'Seltzer? Did you add seltzer to the cognac?'

Reilly shook his head. He gripped the edge of the bed and fixed his gaze firmly on Axel's face, which was no longer white with anger, but red with astonishment.

'You shouldn't have touched the cognac,' Reilly said.

Axel lifted the Viking ship and read the label. Then he sniffed the glass. 'It tasted salty,' he said.

'We have a problem now,' Reilly said.

Axel licked his lips.

'That cognac was meant for me,' Reilly said. 'It was laced with drugs.'

He held his breath. He was uncertain about what would happen next. It was a large dosage, and he had hoped that it might take him all the way to heaven, or hell – if that was where he belonged, he wasn't sure – but he wanted to confess and then he wanted to be gone. Axel disappeared into the bathroom. He turned on the taps. Nothing happened for a while, then Reilly heard dry retching. Then the sound of someone falling over followed by violent thrashing and some rasping noises, which suggested that the overdose was inducing respiratory failure. He thought he heard the towel rack being knocked over, too, and more noise ensued. Reilly sat on his bed, waiting. He felt broken as though they were both taking a beating. It went on for a long time. There seemed to be so much life trying to leave Axel's large body. When it finally grew quiet, he went downstairs to collect the dead kitten.

Afterwards he sat at the kitchen table holding the old Enfield revolver. He remembered when they played spin the bottle as children, and a funny idea came to him. He spun the revolver and it stopped with the barrel pointing at the window. He spun it again. This time the revolver pointed towards the bathroom. He was about to spin it for a third time when he decided to check the chambers.

They were empty.

He had wrapped the dead kitten in a towel. The bundle lay in front of him on the table. He watched the light change outside, saw black clouds gather and block out the sun, and he felt the kitchen grow cooler. But he did not stir from his chair. Every now and then he patted the tiny bundle in the towel. As far as he was concerned, the sun could go down for ever and darkness could cover the earth, he no longer cared. It was the sound of the doorbell that roused him from his apathy. He got up to open the door immediately. He knew they had come for him. It was a relief to move around, a relief to hear voices. That same day Philip Reilly made a full confession.

CHAPTER 35

Irene Selmer was used to getting her own way.

So was Axel Frimann.

'I'm not a taxi,' he said. 'I have to give Jon and Reilly a lift and that's more than enough. Nattmål is completely out of my way, and it's really late.'

Jon cautiously intervened. His feeble appeal had little impact on Axel. 'Surely we could make a small detour,' he suggested. 'It wouldn't be the end of the world. Perhaps his parents are waiting up for him.'

Axel looked at Irene. 'You let him in to your party,' he said, 'so he's your responsibility. You can't expect your guests to run a minicab service in the middle of the night.'

'Stop being such a tosser,' she said. 'You'll drive Kim home and you'll do it now!'

Their shouting made Kim lift his head, but he was far too drunk to realise that the argument was about him.

Jon intervened for a second time. 'It's really not a problem to make that detour, Axel. I think we should get him home.'

Irene tried a different tack. 'Please,' she begged. 'Waking up with a stranger in your house is so awful, I just can't bear it.'

'What's in it for me?' Axel said.

Irene groaned. 'Nothing at all. Does there always have to be something in it for you?'

They lifted Kim and dragged him through the snow. With some effort they reached Axel's Mercedes. Axel looked through the windows at the white leather interior.

'How are you doing, Kim?'

Kim collapsed across the bonnet. He started to hiccup.

'You're not going to throw up, are you?'

Axel looked inside his car again. He made a decision.

'No bloody way am I letting a pissed Chinese guy into my car,' he said. 'He's going to be sick all over the place. He'll ruin the seats. We'll put him in the boot.'

Reilly shook his head in disbelief. 'The boot, are you serious? No, you have got to be joking.'

'Come here,' Axel said. 'Give me a hand.'

'Surely that's not wise?' Jon said.

'I'm not very wise this late at night,' Axel said.

Kim protested a little when they picked him up and put him in the boot, but then he seemed content once more. He curled up and closed his eyes. Perhaps he hadn't even noticed the lid slamming shut. It began to snow. Small, dry flakes which danced in the headlights. Reilly closed his eyes. After the uproar at Irene's, the silence was welcome. The only sound was the constant spinning of the engine. Axel Frimann was driving, Jon dozed on the back seat. Reilly looked forward to being back in his own bed. The many hours of loud music had made him feel dizzy. They were approaching the town. At a roundabout they debated which exit to take.

'I wonder why they come here,' Axel said.

Reilly gave him a quizzical look. 'Who?'

'All the foreigners.'

'It's obvious why they want to come here,' Reilly said. 'Norway's a much better country. Is that so hard to understand?'

'But it's so cold here,' Axel said. 'Look.'

He pointed to the display on the dashboard. 'It's minus seventeen.'

'I don't suppose they worry about the cold,' Reilly said. 'They want food and a job. They want the freedom that we have. They want to be able to walk in the street without having to show ID papers and all that. They want to say what they want and write what they want. It's not like that everywhere, as you well know. Of course people want to come here.'

'That guy in the boot,' Axel said. 'Why do you think he came here?'

'I guess he came with his parents,' Reilly suggested. 'And they probably came here to get a job. And a house. The kind of things people normally want.' He turned and checked the back seat. 'Are you asleep, Jon?'

When they reached Nattmål, Axel pulled up by the letterboxes. He stepped out into the snow, which squeaked underneath his shoes, and some tiny snowflakes landed in his brown hair. Jon woke up and rubbed his eyes.

Icy air poured into the car.

Axel opened the boot.

'We're here,' he called out. 'Out you come!'

Reilly came to help. He slipped a couple of times, and had to hold on to the car for support.

'Look at his eyes,' Axel said. 'Something's wrong with them.'

Reilly leaned over to have a look. 'He's lying on his back,' he said. 'That's not good.'

'Surely it makes no bloody difference which way he's lying,' Axel barked. 'Let's get him out.'

He bent over Kim Van Chau to get a better look at him.

'Hey, Kim. Wake up, damn you!'

Nothing happened in the boot. They started prodding him. Axel slapped him gently across the face, but to no effect. He was still. Reilly started pacing up and down in the snow. His long coat flapped around his legs.

'Do you think he's passed out?'

Axel snarled at him. 'Of course he has. He's not responding.'

'Do you know any first aid?' Reilly asked. 'Like CPR?'

'Why do we need to do CPR?' Axel said. 'He's just had a few too many beers. No one's ever died from that. We need to get him out of the car. Out into the fresh air. Then he'll come round. Right, come on.'

They got hold of Kim. His body was limp like a rag doll, only much heavier.

Jon came to help.

'What's going on?' he asked. 'Can't he walk on his own? Will we have to carry him?'

Axel got Kim out on to the snow. His legs refused to support him and he collapsed on the ground.

'Kim!' Axel shouted. 'Listen to me. You need to stand up.'

Kim Van Chau stayed where he was.

'We've had enough,' Axel continued. 'This isn't a game. Your mum's expecting you.'

'We've done it this time,' Reilly groaned.

'We haven't done shit,' Axel raged.

Jon moaned and fell to his knees. 'We need to call someone,' he gasped. 'We need someone to help us!'

Axel looked hard at both of them. 'We need to talk about this. Now calm down.'

'We'll carry him up to the houses,' Reilly suggested. 'He's bound to have a key in his pocket. We'll let him in and leave him in the hall.'

'We don't even know where he lives,' Axel protested. 'We don't know which house number. Jon, go and read the names on the letterboxes over there. Quickly!'

Jon rushed over, but it was dark and he found it difficult to read most of the names.

'Look out for anyone Vietnamese,' Reilly shouted.

'But they're all foreign,' Jon replied. 'There's not a single one with a Norwegian name. Shall I run up and read the names by the doorbells?'

'Stay here,' Axel thundered. 'We need to stick together.'

'He's not breathing,' Reilly whispered. 'Look at his lips. They've gone blue.'

'That's because it's so cold,' Axel declared. He started walking. He stopped after a few metres, turned abruptly and came back.

'Help me!' he said. 'We need to talk.'

Together they managed to lift Kim into the boot. Axel slammed it shut. He ordered them back inside the car. A few minutes later he started driving.

'We can't stay here,' he explained. 'People can see us. We need time.'

Jon stared out of the rear window. He watched the letterboxes vanish in the darkness.

'But where are we going?' he asked. 'What are we going to do?'

Axel did not have a plan. He drove aimlessly. As long as they kept on moving, a solution would appear, he thought, or the person in the boot would come back to life and start banging on the metal. Time itself would come to their rescue. Nature was playing a nasty trick on them, that was all, so he carried on driving. They passed no one. A Shell petrol station tempted them with hot food and drinks behind lit-up windows. Jon begged Axel to stop.

'People will see us and remember us,' he argued. 'We're not stopping anywhere, not yet.'

'Then when will we be stopping?' Jon persevered. 'Are we going to drive until morning?'

'You're low on petrol,' Reilly remarked. He pointed to the petrol gauge.

Axel Frimann sat hunched over the wheel as though he was steering a ship through a storm. They were moving, but they were not going home. They were in no man's land.

'We might have been mistaken,' Reilly tried. 'Shouldn't we stop to see how he is? If he's come round?'

Axel pulled over at a bus stop.

He opened the door and got out. Reilly staggered after him.

'He's starting to grow cold,' Reilly said. 'It's not necessarily our fault. Perhaps he had a bad heart.'

'Do you know something?' Axel said. 'That's not a risk I'm willing to take.'

They continued to drive through the darkness. At first in huge circles around the town, later along the main road. It was still snowing.

'We need to call,' Jon stuttered.

'It's too late,' Reilly said. 'He's dead.'

'But how?' Jon asked.

'Perhaps he threw up,' Reilly said.

'People don't die from that,' Axel argued.

'Yes. He threw up and inhaled his own vomit. You can drown that way, it does happen.'

Jon curled up on the back seat. He listened to the two men in the front. A few words reached him through the darkness of the car, such as 'it's no good, we can't drive back and leave him at the side of the road, you know that.'

'But he's in the boot now and it's not like he's going to go away.'

'We need to find another solution.'

'It's not our fault.'

'Yes,' Reilly said. 'It is our fault. You and your seats.'

'So it's my fault now, is it? Is that what you're saying? That he drank too much and decided to die in my car? Is that my fault?'

Axel's strong, argumentative voice. Reilly's weak protests.

'It'll only get worse,' Reilly said.

'It can't get any worse,' Axel said.

Twenty minutes later Axel parked the car by the shore of Glitter Lake.

'Why are we stopping?' Jon asked.

'The petrol light has come on,' Axel replied.

The headlights formed two pale blue cones across the ice. After some time they got out of the car and wandered up and down along the shore.

'We can't drive back,' Axel said. 'And we can't take him home with us. This much I assume we do agree on.'

He looked across the ice. To the right of the beach lay a hill with some bushes growing around it.

'There,' Axel said. 'Under the bushes. We'll hide him there, and when the ice melts he'll go through.'

'You're not serious?' Reilly said.

Axel opened the boot.

Jon protested. 'We don't need to say that we put him in the boot,' he wailed. 'Can't we just keep quiet about that bit?'

'They'll find out eventually,' Axel said. 'We'll be convicted of manslaughter. We'll go to prison for several years.'

Jon carried on crying.

'You need to think of those closest to you now,' Axel said. 'Not strangers from a foreign country who decide to die on your doorstep. What do you think your mum will say if you go to jail?'

'But we won't go to jail, will we?' Jon whispered.

'Yes, we will, and I'm not going to let that happen to me. We need to agree a story.'

Jon was still sobbing. He started kicking the tyres of the car. 'Reilly,' he howled. 'Say something!'

Reilly took a few steps through the snow, still keeping his back to him.

Axel pulled out his mobile from his pocket.

'Here you are, Jon, go on, make the call. After all, you're so much better than us. Do the right thing and ruin the rest of your life.'

CHAPTER 36

Ingerid Moreno spotted the taxi from her window.

She pulled on her boots and had just got outside when Yoo Van Chau's foot appeared below the door of the taxi. Yoo was carrying a big shoulder bag. It was heavy, and it upset her balance. The street had been gritted, but there were still icy patches on the flagstone path leading up to the house.

'Let me help you,' Ingerid said.

Yoo hooked her arm through Ingerid's and together they staggered up the slippery flagstones like two old ladies. They could not help but laugh at themselves, and their laughter reminded them of the old life they had lost.

'Please sit down,' Ingerid said, once they got inside.

She had cleaned the house. She had bought flowers and lit candles. She had cooked dinner and set the table, and she had opened a bottle of wine.

Yoo sat on the sofa and Ingerid let herself fall into a chair. There were things that needed saying. They both summoned their courage.

'I'm not making excuses for Jon,' Ingerid began. 'He should have held his ground even though Axel and Reilly were older and stronger than him. But I was young myself once. We went to parties every Saturday and we used to get quite drunk. Some mornings I would wake up unable to recall the night before. It would just be a blur.'

Yoo listened with the shoulder bag on her lap.

'There's so much we don't know about ourselves,' Ingerid said. 'Perhaps we ought to thank fate for the trials we never have to face.'

'Kim shouldn't have drunk as much as he did,' Yoo said. 'He wasn't used to it. I feel sorry for both of them. And I feel sorry for us.'

She looked at the flowers on the table. She recognised them as caramel roses. Ingerid had food in the oven too. She could hear hot fat spitting.

'Every day I light a candle on his grave,' she said. 'I go there whatever the weather, come rain or come shine. Afterwards, I wait for the bus, in the freezing cold. I'm so tired of it. Then I make up my mind not to go the next day, but I think I can hear him calling out for me, so I have to go anyway even though it's cold. I have to, otherwise I can't sleep.'

'He's controlling you,' Ingerid said. 'Did he control you when he was alive as well?'

'Of course not.'

'So why do you allow him to do so now?' She went to the window and looked outside. 'The snow will come soon,' she said. 'Think about that.'

Yoo thought about the snow. It would cover the graves like a duvet.

Ingerid went to the bookcase, pulled out a photo album with a black cover and placed it on the table. 'You first,' she said.

Yoo opened her shoulder bag. Her photo album was pale blue and bore the following title: *My little baby.*

She opened the first page and pointed to the photo of a newborn baby swaddled in a blanket.

'Kim,' she whispered. 'On the day he was born.'

CHAPTER 37

Reilly's cell measured eight square metres. It had a simple bed and a desk, and he had his own toilet. He also had a shelf with a handful of books, and on the wall above his bed he had fixed an old photo of himself, Axel and Jon when they were boys. Axel's father had taken the picture. It was before the stroke destroyed him. Axel was wearing a white shirt and jeans; Jon was in shorts and on his head he wore the dark blue cap from Toten Transport. Reilly himself was wearing an old tracksuit with red and blue trim.

Reilly studied the picture every day. He was convinced that he would eventually spot signs of everything that had happened since then. A shadow, perhaps, or a certain light. But he found no such thing. They were just little kids with skinny legs and pointy knees.

The window of his cell faced the river, and a herd of cows was grazing on its bank. There were fifty, maybe sixty animals there, and he enjoyed watching them. The animals were sturdy and shaggy, some were as pale as cream, others black or red, and they always moved as one. Whenever it began to rain, they would huddle together under a cluster of trees in a compact slumbering mass.

'Herefordshire,' Hermansen said.

Hermansen was the prison guard whom Reilly liked the most. He was the oldest one on the section and would retire shortly. Sometimes you could sense that he was already winding down. He had lost some of his flexibility, and his dealings with the inmates was characterised by a brutal honesty.

'Herefordshire,' Reilly echoed. 'You know about cows then?'

'I know the farmer,' Hermansen said. 'It's the best meat there is.'

Reilly remained by the window. He was filled with a sense of gravity, which pulled him towards the floor, but it was not unpleasant. It was the feeling of being in the right place. I'm atoning now, he thought. I atone while I sleep, and every second I repay part of a huge debt.

'Are they outside in the winter?' he asked, nodding towards the cows.

'Oh, no,' Hermansen said. 'They go back in the cowshed at the first snowfall.'

'But that could be any minute,' Reilly said. 'We're halfway through November. What will I look at then?'

'Then you'll have to look at the sky,' Hermansen said. 'And the clouds. You'll always find something to look at. You have to. You're going to be here a long time.'

Reilly went to his bed. He sat down and picked up the Koran that was lying on the blanket.

The older man watched him kindly. 'Is there anything else I can do for you?'

'I've been thinking about something,' Reilly said, 'since you're asking. I was wondering if perhaps I should send flowers. To Ingerid and to Yoo Van Chau.'

Hermansen frowned. 'Flowers? What good would that do?'

'I just want to express my grief. At everything that happened.'

'For what you've done,' Hermansen corrected him.

Reilly nodded. 'Yes. For what I've done.'

'I don't think that's a very good idea,' Hermansen said. 'It won't solve anything.'

'But I have to do something,' Reilly groaned. 'You understand that, don't you?'

'You can't send flowers,' Hermansen said. 'They don't want to hear from you ever again. Leave them in peace.'

Reilly slumped on the bed. The Koran slipped out of his hand on to the blanket.

'No matter how bad your actions were,' Hermansen said, 'in the end you confessed. That in itself is an act of decency.'

The door to his cell slammed loudly behind him. Reilly was on the verge of tears. If only I could get high, he thought, a seductive little drop of Salty Water. He opened the Koran and picked out a verse at random.

If a man kills a believer intentionally, his recompense is Hell, to abide therein for ever: And the wrath and the curse of God are upon him, and a dreadful penalty is prepared for him.

He returned to the window and focused on the cows again. Big, beautiful and slow they meandered across the meadow, seemingly unaffected by time or man, enclosed in a world of their own, devoid of any urgency. Only a couple of calves that did not know any better leapt and gambolled around. A few hard kicks from the older animals quickly put them in their place.

CHAPTER 38

Jon is waiting.

From the steps outside the ward he has a good view of the area in front of the hospital. He is sitting on the third step and though the sun is shining, he is warmly dressed because it is September and the nights can be chilly. Any second now Axel's green Mercedes will appear around the bend. While he waits, he chews his nails. He has bitten them right down. The tips of his fingers are red and sore. He thinks about everything that has happened and about how he is going to move on. He knows he has to make a choice. That's why I'm struggling, he thinks, because I can't make up my mind. But sometimes we need to face reality. And perhaps that is not fair, but nothing about this situation is fair. It's best to keep my mouth shut, he thinks, I'm protecting Axel and Reilly. They are my friends, and we're in this together for ever.

Molly Gram appears from around the corner. Melis is leaping and bouncing. Jon raises his hand to greet her.

'Are you leaving?' she asks. 'Are they coming to fetch you?'

He kicks the step. Her gaze makes him feel giddy.

'So when are you back, then? Sunday evening?'

He nods. Her irises light up like gemstones inside the black make-up. Her eyes appear shiny and wet. But then again the air is sharp, he thinks. I mustn't jump to conclusions.

Axel's green Mercedes pulls up outside the hospital.

All of a sudden Jon is consumed by fear at having to leave Molly so soon after he has found her and she has set something in motion. Axel beeps the horn. Due to the reflection from the windscreen, Jon cannot see his face, but Reilly gets out of the car. The wind grabs hold of his coat, and makes him look like a gigantic fluttering moth.

'Text me,' Molly says.

Quick as lightning she comes over and kisses him on the lips.

Jon starts to walk, but he would rather stay where he is, so he slows his pace and turns around one last time. Axel is always on the lookout, he thinks. He keeps an eye on me. And Reilly always recites threats from the Koran. As long as they leave me in peace, as long as my anxiety doesn't get the better of me, then I'll be all right.

'Jon Moreno,' Molly calls out. 'Cheer up. It's not like you're going to your own execution!'

He feels light-hearted again. I think I've got myself a girlfriend, he concludes. I do believe I have a girlfriend.

Axel beeps the horn again.

And Jon starts to run.